# and the earth drank deep & Other Stories

WINNERS OF THE COMMONWEALTH SHORT STORY PRIZE 2022

# and the earth drank deep
## & Other Stories

WINNERS OF THE COMMONWEALTH
SHORT STORY PRIZE 2022

**and the earth drank deep & Other Stories:**
**Winners of the Commonwealth Short Story Prize 2022**

This edition has been published in 2022
in the United Kingdom by Paper + Ink.

**www.paperand.ink**
Twitter: @paper_andink
Instagram: paper_and.ink



1 2 3 4 5 6 7 8 9 10

ISBN 9781911475620

A CIP catalogue record for this book is available from the British Library.
Jacket design by James Nunn: www.jamesnunn.co.uk | @Gnunkse
Printed and bound in Great Britain.

# CONTENTS

# ABOUT THE COMMONWEALTH SHORT STORY PRIZE

The Commonwealth Short Story Prize is administered by the Commonwealth Foundation. Now in its eleventh year, the prize is awarded for the best piece of unpublished short fiction (2,000 – 5,000 words). Regional winners receive GBP 2,500, and the overall winner receives GBP 5,000. It is free to enter and open to citizens of all the countries of the Commonwealth. Entries can be submitted in Bengali, Chinese, English, French, Greek, Malay, Portuguese, Samoan, Swahili, Tamil and Turkish, as well as the Creole languages of the Commonwealth. They can also be translated into English from any language. The international panel of judges selects one winner from each of the five Commonwealth regions – Africa, Asia,

Canada and Europe, Caribbean and the Pacific – one of whom is chosen as the overall winner.

### CSSP 2022 Judging Panel

Chair: Fred D'Aguiar
Africa: Louise Umutoni-Bower
Asia: Jahnavi Barua
Canada and Europe: Stephanos Stephanides
Caribbean: Kevin Jared Hosein
Pacific: Jeanine Leane

## About the Commonwealth Foundation

The Commonwealth Foundation is an intergovernmental organisation established by Member States of the Commonwealth. The Foundation works to support civil-society engagement in shaping the policies and decisions that affect people's lives. Its cultural programming is founded on the belief that well-told stories can help people make sense of events and take action to bring about change. The

Foundation works with local and international partners to identify and deliver a wide range of cultural projects and platforms, including adda, an online magazine of new writing.

**www.commonwealthfoundation.com**
**www.addastories.org**

# and the earth drank deep

## NTSIKA KOTA

Cool morning air rushed into and out of the hunter's lungs. The still dew-damp grass wet his legs to the thighs as he charged through it. His prey, a nyala, was fleeing right into the path of the rest of the party, downwind and invisible in the tall grass. As the panicked animal fled, the hunter watched a single spear arc gracefully aloft and find its mark in the nyala's flank. The beast continued to run, its pace steadily slowing until it fell to the ground.

In the excitement of his first real hunt, he was the quickest to reach the downed animal. The young man was surprised to find it was still alive, breathing heavily, a muddy pool of blood already forming. He looked into its bovine eyes, which were filled with exhausted panic. Or resignation. He wasn't sure. But he was drawn to it. The pain.

The suffering. He found his own breathing was harder now than before, and his heart was pounding. He reached for the shaft of the spear buried in bloodied flesh and twisted it gently, rapt as the eyes widened and the nyala let out a weak grunt of pain.

His attention completely focused on the wounded animal at his feet, the hunter reached over with his other hand to get a better grip on the spear. He was startled out of his trance by a quick thrust of another spear directly into the nyala's heart. It stopped moving immediately. He looked up and saw Zungu staring back with a mixture of disapproval and irritation. Zungu scolded him for letting the beast suffer, implying that he must not have been ready to join a true hunt. The hunter apologised, showing sufficient deference to cover up – he hoped – the enjoyment that must have been plastered all over his face just seconds before.

The rest of the party soon joined them and they set about gutting their kill, removing the offal with sharpened stone knives before mounting the carcass on a long yoke for the trek home. By the time they were done and ready to head back, the sun was approaching zenith, bringing with it the biting heat of summer. The party began the return journey with Zungu leading them in a victory song. They left the pile of offal for scavengers to find.

In the monotony of the march back, the hunter relived the nyala's death over and over again in his mind. He could smell its blood whenever the wind blew right, but now that it was meat, it was of little interest to him. The more he thought about it, the more he realised that his fascination came from seeing the essence of life extinguished: the fear and confusion and pain. He had seen death before – during funeral rites in seasons past – but he only now made the connection between the two. *Life and death. Death and dying.* He eagerly looked forward to the next hunt.

When they got back to the camp, the junior members of the hunting party were instructed to begin preparing the meat to be cooked and preserved. The seniors headed to Ndvuna Nyathi's hut to relax with *buganu* brew and bid the sun farewell. As he was leaving, Zungu instructed the hunter to gather wood and kindling for the cooking fire. A child's job. Without waiting for a reply, Zungu turned and went on his way. The hunter regarded Zungu's back with a baleful glare, then stormed out of the encampment. He had no intention of gathering fuelwood.

He made his way down the rise on which the encampment sat. He intended to wander among the trees at the base of the hill and find somewhere to sulk until the food was prepared. Before he reached the treeline, commotion and sounds of distress caught his attention. Out of the brush burst a group of four young women from the settlement. Two of them were helping along a third, her arms draped over their shoulders for support. Her leg was bleeding profusely below the knee, and she couldn't place any weight on it. The fourth was behind them, carrying a large branch and frequently casting nervous glances over her shoulder.

The hunter would have avoided the women and let somebody else deal with the matter, but on the open path, they immediately caught sight of him. He knew he couldn't ignore them now without fairly serious consequences to his social standing. He arranged his face into a sufficiently concerned expression and rushed to help. To speed up their progress, he lifted the injured woman in his arms and rushed up the rise to the encampment. He carried her directly to the *nyanga's* hut, then loitered for the appropriate length of time to show concern. Her shouts of pain soon attracted Nyathi's and the other men's attention. They made their way to the *nyanga's* hut to enquire. The hut was soon far too crowded, so the *nyanga* sent everyone away except one of the injured young woman's friends.

Outside, the other two young women, now calmer, explained to Nyathi and the gathered curious what had happened. Their party had been attacked by a jackal, apparently unprovoked, while they were gathering berries and roots from a particularly productive grove. Together, they had managed to scare off the animal with noise and kicks, but not before it had bitten one of them quite badly. There were murmurs of worry that the animal might have been afflicted with water-madness. It would need to be dealt with before it struck again, or passed its madness onto other beasts in the area.

The implications for the young woman in the hut went unspoken.

Nyathi quieted the crowd, then asked the young women patiently if they had seen the tell-tale white saliva on the creature's mouth. Neither could say for sure, pleading that the entire incident had happened too quickly for them to remember many details. The hunter, who had slowly been making his way to the edge of the crowd, happened to glance across and catch Zungu's gaze. The other man did not break eye contact. The hunter, thoroughly irritated by Zungu's endless condescension, decided to do something about it.

The discussion turned to the question of who should form the hunting party to remove this threat. If the animal was indeed afflicted, it would be exceedingly dangerous. The hunter raised his hand and volunteered, staring directly at Zungu. The other's features remained an inscrutable mask. The hunter only broke eye contact when he turned to answer Nyathi's question. The young man assured the *ndvuna* that he understood what he was volunteering for, but that he wanted to protect his people. He added a smile to convey youthful bravery.

Nyathi nodded. Then, speaking to the rest, he asked for another volunteer to join the hunt. A man soon spoke up: Mvubu, one of the oldest who still hunted. He had been a quiet man since losing his wife and infant in childbirth many seasons earlier, and had never taken another wife. The hunter did not know Mvubu well, and didn't particularly care one way or another who joined him – as long as it was not Zungu.

With limited time until the sun sank below the horizon, Mvubu and the hunter quickly gathered up their weapons and headed down the hill at a run, following directions to the grove given them by the gatherers. Mvubu volunteered no conversation, and the hunter was happy to keep the silence. The only sound he could hear was the wind rushing by his ears, and his own breathing.

At their pace, it didn't take them long to reach the grove. They stopped and assessed the situation. The warm air carried the distinct smell of jackal droppings. Mvubu was a much more experienced tracker, and he soon found the traces left by the fleeing group earlier that day. He signalled the hunter and they worked backwards, spears at the ready, ears alert for any sound in the still air. From where the trail of blood started, Mvubu walked carefully in a growing spiral, seeking the signs of the jackal's retreat. He soon found them, and again quietly signalled to the hunter to follow.

Then the silence was broken by a low, menacing growl coming from a small den well hidden amidst some bushes. A jackal crawled out from under the vegetation. Its abdomen was distended, and it seemed barely able to stand. Its countenance was nevertheless writ with the deadly determination of a mother protecting her young.

Realising what must have happened earlier in the day, Mvubu and the hunter retraced their steps, moving away from the den slowly and deliberately. They made sure to avoid making eye contact, or any kind of noise. The mother jackal remained on guard, teeth bared until she judged they understood the score; then she once more lay down heavily, watchful.

Eventually, Mvubu turned to the hunter to suggest they head back and report their findings – but suddenly, a brown blur burst forth from the bushes behind him and charged into his legs. This second jackal was on top of Mvubu in an instant. Once he was on the ground, it latched onto the wrist of his spear hand and began shaking it, while pulling his arm outstretched. He screamed in pain and tried to beat it back with the shield in his other hand, but it was no use. Their struggle kicked up dust from tufty ground.

The enraged jackal was intent on maiming him. Mvubu shouted for help, but the hunter stood by, transfixed by the spectacle. He felt his skin tingling with excitement. With great effort, Mvubu finally fought his way into a prostrate position, trying to stand up. The jackal saw its opportunity and struck. It relinquished its grip on Mvubu's wrist and charged for his neck with a snarl. The force of its charge once again knocked Mvubu to the ground. He tried to fight it off, but with his shield arm pinned under him, his efforts were of little use.

Seeing that the jackal was completely focused on Mvubu, the hunter rammed his spear into its heart. It yelped briefly, and was still. He switched his attention back to Mvubu. The man tried to speak, but his mangled throat did not allow it. The hunter did not say anything. Mvubu tried to stand, but was too weak, and fell back into the muddy puddle of blood that had formed beneath him. He stared up at the hunter in confusion. His eyes asked why. He saw no reply in the hunter's face, only naked excitement. The coughing and gurgling of his breathing soon quieted to nothing. The hunter crouched down and brought his face close to Mvubu's, watching. Waiting for the last blink.

When it was over, the hunter lifted Mvubu onto his shoulder and began the journey back to the settlement, holding his own shield and bloodied spear in one hand. He marched as quickly as he could while carrying Mvubu's weight, not wanting to navigate in darkness.

Sensing the death of her mate, the mother jackal howled her grief into the cooling evening air.

• • •

Despite his best efforts, the sun was on the horizon before the hunter reached the settlement, and it was getting dark. Carrying Mvubu's lifeless weight was more tiring that he had anticipated, and he had been forced to stop frequently to rest. He had considered leaving the corpse behind, but knew that social convention prohibited such a thing unless his own circumstances were truly dire. He would lose much respect. It would invalidate any acclaim he was due for killing the jackal. So he marched on, determined.

All the colour drained from the land as the sun set, leaving only shades of darkness. In the failing light, he could still make out familiar landmarks, and realised he wasn't far now. Once on clear ground, he knew it would be no struggle to follow the light from the firepit. If it came to it, the hunter knew he could also wait until the stars came out to guide him. As it turned out, neither was necessary. Once he was out onto clear ground, he could hear sounds of conversation carried faintly on the cold night air.

After one final rest, the hunter began the climb up the dark flank of the hill to the settlement. As he drew near, the smell of cooking meat triggered a flood of saliva in his mouth, and he noticed how hungry he was. And tired. He finally made it into the encampment and headed toward the *nyanga's* hut. The *nyanga* would need to begin preparing funeral rites. He took a circuitous route, avoiding the central firepit and the crowd around it. If they saw Mvubu's corpse, their attention would immediately be focused there, he thought, and not on the fact that he alone had slain the jackal.

When the hunter reached the *nyanga's* hut, the young woman who had been bitten was asleep, and the *nyanga* was changing the poultice on her wound. The hunter put Mvubu's stiffening body down on the floor; then the *nyanga* waved him off without a word. The hunter did not have opportunity to tell the *nyanga* that the jackal did not have water-madness. He shrugged and left the hut, making sure to take his shield and bloodied spear with him.

He paused for a second, deciding what the correct course of action was, then he made his way to Nyathi's hut to report Mvubu's death. The hunter had never been inside the elder's hut – his status was far too low for that. He stood outside and hailed the leader. A conversation inside stopped mid-sentence, and he heard Nyathi's voice give him permission to enter. He stepped past the threshold and was immediately displeased to see a scowling Zungu. He kept his features neutral with a hint of sorrow as he reported Mvubu's death from the jackal attack.

The hunter recounted the event, carefully adjusting his tale to conceal his own culpability in Mvubu's death. He focused his telling on the attack on Mvubu. Then, when Nyathi asked about the jackal, the hunter was able to mention in an off-handed way – as if he had forgotten – that he had slain it. When the old man asked whether the beast had appeared water-mad or not, the hunter paused as if his whole account had not been mentally rehearsed multiple times. He told the truth: it had not been water-mad, but defensive of its den-mate and newborn pups. Nyathi applauded his bravery in killing the jackal and his sense of duty in bringing Mvubu's body. Then the elder dismissed him, advising him to get himself some food. Zungu remained silent.

When the hunter departed, Zungu listened for the sound of his footsteps moving away. Then he asked Nyathi for leave to go to the site of Mvubu's death. He wished to retrieve the fallen man's spear and shield to be buried with him, as was customary. Nyathi's wrinkled face broke out into a smile and he commended his protégé's sense of duty. However, he told the younger man that such things were the duty of elders. At Zungu's protest that the distance was too great, Nyathi merely raised a gently silencing hand. He assured Zungu that age had not yet taken the last of his strength. Knowing that the matter was settled, Zungu pressed no further and allowed Nyathi to guide their discussion onto other topics.

On the other side of the settlement, at the firepit, the hunter was quickly surrounded by people wanting to find out what had happened. He was happy to oblige, making sure always to show the appropriate level of sorrow for Mvubu. By the time the fire had burned down to embers late that night, he had told and retold his sanitised version of events many times, and cemented his place as a hero – at least among his peers. The hunter retired that night with a satisfied smile on his face, replaying in his mind the thrill of that afternoon.

At first light the next day, Nyathi set out for the site of Mvubu's demise. He still clearly remembered the directions that the young women had given. He was confident he could get there and back easily before the storm that was threatening rolled in.

Nyathi did not have any trouble locating Mvubu's and the hunter's tracks once he was near the grove. He immediately spotted the dead jackal lying on the ground. A cloud of flies buzzed around the neat wound in its side. Nyathi quickly located Mvubu's shield and spear.

He was about to leave when something about the scene caught his attention. He surveyed the area more closely. He wasn't sure what had caused him to pause.

Using Mvubu's spear, he levered the jackal's stiff carcass up to look at the other wounds the hunter had presumably inflicted. There were none that he could spot in the animal's blood-matted fur. He looked more closely, and satisfied himself that there were indeed no wounds besides the single one its sunward flank: one very neat wound, the result of extraordinary luck or skill – or an unmoving target.

He crouched to try and read the story in the earth of what had happened, and chided himself for having thoughtlessly trampled some of the tracks. Fortunately, there were enough left that he could make a reasonable guess. Recalling where he had picked up Mvubu's discarded weapons, he was able to spot where the jackal's claws had torn up the ground as it charged from behind a nearby bush at Mvubu. That explained the positioning of the spear, which he replaced as close as he could to its original position.

Now fully engrossed, Nyathi carefully searched the area for human tracks – the hunter's – tearing up the ground, sprinting to Mvubu's aid. He found none. He decided to try another tack. Still holding the shield, he replaced it approximately where it had fallen. He guessed that Mvubu had been able to keep it on his arm because of the leather straps, unlike the spear, which he had dropped. Using the shield as a guide, Nyathi tried to imagine the position in which Mvubu had been fighting. He thought the blood coating the edge of the face-down shield must have been Mvubu's own, from trying to fight the animal off. From the sheer amount of blood on the ground and coating the jackal's maw, Nyathi judged that the animal had almost certainly taken hold of Mvubu's neck. He would have been utterly helpless.

Feeling a lump form in his throat, Nyathi gathered up the spear and shield and left the grove without a backward glance, curiosity driven from his mind. He felt the weight of death press on his chest.

By the time Nyathi returned to the settlement, heavy, dark clouds had rolled into the sky. The breeze brought with it the dusty, sharp smell of a brewing storm. Nyathi headed straight for the *nyanga's* hut to return the shield and spear to their fallen wielder. Inside, he found the *nyanga* struggling to manoeuvre Mvubu's stiff body into a more serene supine position. Nyathi was ill-prepared for the sight of Mvubu's mangled neck and still-open eyes, and gasped. No matter how many times he was forced to confront it, Nyathi was still sometimes caught unawares by the spectre of death.

The *nyanga* took the shield and spear from Nyathi, and commiserated with him. Mvubu's injuries were severe. The *nyanga* judged that although the damage to his wrist might – alone – have been survivable, Mvubu surely would have succumbed to water-madness in any case. Perhaps in the end, he mused, this had been a kinder death. Nyathi was about to correct him, realising that he must not yet have heard the news that the jackal had not been water-mad after all, when a thought struck him mute.

*Injury to the wrist. To the wrist. The wrist.* Why would an attacking predator relinquish a death grip on the neck only to grab onto a limb? Surely it would not, he thought. Suddenly the details came together in Nyathi's mind. He realised that he had failed to find the tracks indicating the hunter's rush to aid Mvubu because the youth had made no such charge. He grasped how the youth had been able to so neatly slay the jackal, and why its lower flank was covered in Mvubu's blood: blood was already on the ground when the jackal died. He had already been twice injured and bleeding by the time the boy had slain the attacker. The hunter must have delayed. That was not the story he had told.

Righteous anger welled up in Nyathi's chest. The boy had lied. Cleverly, but it was a lie nonetheless. To hide his cowardice, no doubt. Nyathi did not fault the boy for wavering in the face of such danger, but to lie this way to his elders was unacceptable. To spit on the death of a tribesman! The issue would have to be dealt with, and soon. Nyathi left the *nyanga's* hut without another word.

He went directly to his own hut, but not before stopping a passing child. He instructed the child to find Zungu and inform him that he had been summoned. The child, feeling the iron in the old man's voice and in his grip, rushed off to comply without question.

As the storm approached, thunder rumbled ever louder. Rain would fall by evening, Nyathi judged. When Zungu arrived, Nyathi had been ruminating at length and remained of two minds. On one hand, the boy was young. Was it not expected for youths to be egotistical, and to seek to protect their image? On the other hand, what lesson would the young man learn if his duplicity went unchecked? Also to be considered was the effect on the morale of the village as a whole, to know of the true circumstances of Mvubu's death. Nyathi was glad to have a second set of eyes with which to view the problem.

When Nyathi had apprised Zungu of his findings from the scene, and from Mvubu's wounds, the younger man was quiet for some time. Outside, the first large drops began to fall from darkened sky. The trickle quickly grew to a deluge. When Zungu spoke, he had to raise his voice to be heard over the din. He relayed to

Nyathi the incident with the nyala on the day of the boy's first true hunt. At the time – though he had found the boy's behaviour strange – he had dismissed it. Subsequently, when the boy had come to report Mvubu's death, with no blood on his own shield or body, Zungu confessed he had again found it strange ... but had again dismissed it.

In the face of Nyathi's findings, Zungu asserted, the boy's behaviour could no longer be dismissed. The two men discussed the problem into the hours of darkness, stopping only to strike a fat-soaked torch alight. After much discussion, they finally settled on a tentative plan for handling the youth. They would address it after Mvubu's body was returned to the ancestors the following day.

Both feeling a weight off their shoulders, they bid each other goodnight, and Zungu left. Outside, the storm was still at full strength. Zungu paused at the threshold to allow his eyes to adjust to the darkness, then made his way to his hut by the glow of light from nearby huts and the frequent bolts of lightning. Thus distracted, he did not see the single set of quickly disappearing footprints in the mud leading from the front of Nyathi's hut and around the back.

His heart racing at the close call, the hunter took a few deep breaths and then headed to his own hut, feeling grateful for his good fortune. If he had not – on a complete whim – decided to go to Nyathi and offer to retrieve Mvubu's shield and spear, he would never have overheard that conversation. He guessed that he had missed much of the discussion, but he had heard enough to know that he had to act, and quickly. If the news got out to the rest of the settlement, he would be a pariah. He had some thinking to do.

• • •

The thunderstorm lasted well into the night, but by the early hours it had weakened to a light drizzle. The rising sun brought with it a day of great sorrow and tragedy in the life of the small village on the hill. Early that morning, a group of young girls on their way to the river came across the body of Zungu, who had apparently slipped and struck his head on a sharp outcropping of rock.

One of the girls, distraught, had rushed to Nyathi's hut to report the death, but he did not reply to her hails from outside. Knowing she was not allowed inside, she rushed to inform the *nyanga*. He went to Zungu's side to examine him, and determined that, indeed, the young man had expired. The *nyanga* sent the girls on their way, and enlisted one of Zungu's peers to carry the body to his hut. Then, feeling puzzled and saddened by the village's recent streak of misfortune, he went to Nyathi's hut to report this latest calamity. He dreaded the task. It was known how fondly Nyathi thought of Zungu. The old man would be devastated.

When Nyathi failed to respond, the *nyanga* stepped inside to wake him. Nyathi was lying on his sleeping mat, with his back to the entrance. The *nyanga* spoke again, quite loudly, but Nyathi did not stir. Strange. With a growing sense of foreboding, the *nyanga* reached out to shake Nyathi awake, grabbing his shoulder. It was cold to the touch. He rolled him onto his back and felt for a heartbeat. Stillness. The *ndvuna*, it seemed, had died in his sleep.

# THE LAST DIVER ON EARTH

## SOFIA MARIAH MA

When they finally found Ibu, she was laid out on the beach.

Draped in a shroud of slimy, rusted kelp, she looked like a giant glutinous rice dessert encased in steamed bamboo leaves. It wasn't unusual that she was naked. Here, we dived naked. Off the coast of the Lesser Sunda Islands. Between the seas of Banda and Flores. But seeing her like this, I remembered Ibu's promise.

She had told me she wanted to be the last freediver on Earth.

She forbade me from going into the water – the water we both love. But who ever really listens to their own mother?

With our lives so intertwined with the sea,

Ibu and I had always lived with death as our fickle, wearisome neighbour. In the good years, death kept to himself. When things were bad, we would see him wandering the coast and picking at debris, at bodies, as in the aftermath of a tsunami.

Sometimes we would see him watching eagerly as sharks prowled the shallow waters near shore for easy pickings – well, not *too* easy, as we Bajau learn to swim before we walk or talk – but easier than, say, venturing into the dark, frigid depths without coming across a meal for weeks. Still, I never expected I would come across my mother's body on land rather than in the sea.

A small crowd had gathered around Ibu by the time I arrived.

No one spoke. No one so much as breathed, as if out of respect for the woman they recognised as their *dukun*, the traditional healer who taught them to harvest remedies from the waters around them.

Need a quick pain reliever? Agitate an ointment from the venom of chestnut-coloured cone snail shells. Want to disinfect a wound?

Cultivate a salve from the vase-shaped glass sponge. Her marine knowledge unparalleled, Ibu seemed chosen by the sea. Its crystalline blue waters formed her skin. Its rippled, foamy white waves like mottled sapphires took the place of her clothes, which kept her warm on stormy days when the water temperatures would drop, drop, drop.

"Rumi."

I knew it was Professor Arisa even before she called me, her stiff, gnarled fingers gripping my shoulder and pinching me right to my bone. Few were convinced that lanky, wiry Arisa, who suffered from severe arthritis, was in her seventies.

She often enlisted Ibu's help, along with her own sensitive hands and inflamed joints, to carry out her research in the twilight zone of the mesophotic reef. This was where sunlight reached its end and the abyss began, and where, if life could resist death's gravity in the deep, it would move to thrive in brighter, warmer oceans. As it was already too expensive to use offshore deep vessels and submersibles to locate and collect samples of new marine species, Arisa was relieved to have found a natural deep diver in Ibu to aid her in discovery, particularly in places that were too erratic, too intricate. Nonetheless, as we dived, scrubbing the bleached reefs or surveying the continental shelf, Arisa always came with us. She, in full diving gear – wetsuit, rebreather, computer; Ibu and I, armed with only our spears and intergenerational map of the sea imprinted into our minds, our muscle memory.

Once, Arisa told us scientists like her had ascertained that our enlarged spleens and specialised eye systems are what enabled us to dive without masks or the need to breathe for long periods of time.

But to us, it was our poverty that had created these material effects.

In fact, if it weren't for Arisa, Ibu wouldn't have been able to raise or educate me, and this made Ibu feel indebted to her. She didn't even mind that once a year, when she was invited to the mainland, to Nusa Baru City on Kalimantan, she was made to act like a sea lion exhibit in an aquarium while Arisa presented papers and published books on the new marine plant and animal species she identified after the Second Deluge at the end of the twenty-second century. Ibu said that Arisa rarely mentioned the ones we could no longer find.

I suppose with Ibu gone now, this debt now falls to me.

"Rumi, get a hold of yourself."

I couldn't.

"Marli's gone."

I didn't stop crying and beating my chest until the sight of Ibu's sickly white, bulbous body, reeking with a sour, putrefying odour, hit me. Yet it was at that moment also that I saw the strange-looking weed – no, seaweed – trapped in her wrinkled, bloated fingers.

At first glance, it appeared typical of green algae. Velvety to the touch, its flat, delicate fronds opened to a fan the size of my palm. Even the mossy-green, threadlike tendrils that barely clung to its frayed edges, as if it had been torn from its source in a hurry, looked normal to me. But the second my eyes saw its inner structure, I knew it was something I had never seen.

Seemingly more akin to a common nerve plant than seaweed, its crimson veins stood out against its olive-green fronds. They were aligned in such a fine, tightly packed mesh, it reminded me of the netting used by the village fishermen. Waking up at dawn, they would cast their nets to trap shrimp or anchovies before the village farmers could start switching on their drones or gathering their seaweed. As Ibu was neither a fisherman nor a farmer, she had no business being so close to the coast or holding onto some seaweed.

*Wait – was that why Ibu was taken?*

She knew our myths, our stories.

Our seas belong to the Queen of the South Seas. To Nyai Lara Kidul, the Protector, the Avenger. If it had been me, Ibu would have castigated me, slapped me, for daring to wear or carry anything green – even a shade of it – without preparing a tribute for the Queen. And there was nothing, *nothing* that Ibu could give, naked and alone, when she chose to return to land with this *weed*. So why did she? Why did she risk inviting Her wrath, Her jealousy? I didn't understand it. I couldn't.

Later, when the village cremated Ibu – coming together, building a bamboo pyre for her and setting her on fire – I went through the motions like a paralytic, like an infected snail with a parasitic worm in my head, shaking hands with every villager who approached me and offered their condolences and their memories of Ibu helping them in some way or another.

Through their words and gestures, I already knew they wanted me to be Ibu – to be what Ibu was for them.

From my mother, I had learned how to swim with the currents and dive far from the village, to such great depths even Arisa was tempted to recruit me. With Ibu, I had stayed in a stilt house so close to the sea that I, too, could warn the villagers about its coming caprices. Its warming surges. Its chilling swells. Its acidifying fluidities.

I, too, could tell them: *Harvest your sea lettuce today. Or get your drones to take them out of the water. Come moonlight, you can put them back into the absurd squares of ocean you think you can control, or own. And don't forget your tributes to Nyai Lara. Yes, yes, flowers would do. Put them out to float in baskets weaved out of bamboo leaves. What? You've forgotten how? Come here, I'll show you. I'll show you how.*

Before she died, Ibu had asked me to follow Arisa back to the mainland, where I could find a job, a life ... and never return.

When I objected, she had laughed. Her tanned, wizened features were strikingly delicate when she smiled. And when she replied, her thin, dark hair and small, hazel eyes bristled, just like mine: "Live, Rumi."

Watching the flames engulf Ibu's body, lapping her up and spreading from end to end of the strips of palm leaves and vines used to bind her body, I told myself that the villagers could have their memory of Ibu as the woman carved by the sea. I will remember her as the woman who carved *me*.

Deeper into the night, when Arisa arrived to take me back to her stilt hut by the beach, the last of the smouldering embers that used to be Ibu died. Opening my mouth to speak, I couldn't help it that my tone was accusatory. I was angry. "*You* did this," I said, looking out to the dark waters lapping around the village and seeing little. "It was you."

"You don't know what you're saying, Rumi."

I knew exactly what I was saying. "It was you who pushed Ibu to dive further ... deeper ..."

"It was not just for me. It's for science ... for everyone," answered Arisa, sounding like one of those ubiquitous holographic advertisements I saw floating along the MagRail tracks in Nusa Baru City. Each and every one of them advocated the green-powered dreams of carbon-free, autonomous transportation and production made reality by developments in solar and biochemical energy sources. All for a better world. A better humanity.

Following Ibu on one of her trips to visit Arisa, I should have been impressed. I should have been amazed by the city's naturally bioluminescent walls, paths and trees at night, allowing its inhabitants to work and play while being swathed in subdued tones of blue, green and white.

But I thought everything – *everything* – Nusa Baru City was built on was owed to the sea.

In school, I had learned that this very trick of light was derived from single-celled dinoflagellates, or plankton, which bloom on coastal waves and glow luminous blue right after sunset. Yet, at same time, I also remembered Ibu telling me how these same surrealistic organisms signalled an omen – a warning from the sea.

She had said: *Rumi, sometimes too much life is too much. Avoid eating any fish in the area. Throw back the crabs, the mussels harvested from this sea, because tomorrow, a red tide will come. A red tide will come.*

At the turn of the twenty-third century, red tides became the norm for most depressed towns and displaced cities such as ours. They brought unnaturally warm currents with too many nutrients, and too many parasites spreading disease among the plankton and all that relied on it – including humans.

Like Rotterdam, Jakarta, too, had attempted to hold back the sea with its own version of the Maeslant Barrier. After it failed, drains and canals were designed and built to turn the area into a 'city of sponge'. It wanted to naturally redistribute floodwater and rainwater away from its low-lying roads and housing areas to its man-made parks and rooftop gardens, as Shanghai had done. Mangroves were replanted. Wetlands were reformed along the tragic coastline of abandoned highways and buildings, looking more and more like a last-ditch attempt to cleanse the city of the failed, embittered concrete nightmares and returning them to the Queen of the South Seas.

But Nyai Lara Kidul had predicaments of her own, too.

All the damage we had wrought on Nature with our fossil fuels and plastics was no longer reversible. Extensive swathes of ocean had been left deoxygenated and dead. Massive volumes of trash and plastic had been regurgitated onto our shores. Still, by 2210, Nusa Baru City was marketing itself as the *real* 'city of the future' on the Kalimantan mainland – a revolutionary capital that would contribute neither carbon nor plastic to the environment. Diving with Ibu and still finding dead zones and currents of plastic wherever we went in the ever-warming sea, we knew that Nusa Baru City would be no different.

When Arisa finally spoke again, she looked distracted. She was sitting on a chair surrounded by stacks of paper filled with numbers and scribbles all around her cluttered hut. Numerous cups of *sopi*, or palm liquor, were poured from bamboo bottles and drained. Her *ikat* skirt spun out of silky golden and red strands was softly shimmering like tessellated gossamer under the full moon.

And for once, Arisa was looking at her computer screens, which were showing changes in sea conditions, and seeing nothing at all. Combing her hands through her hair that shone hoary like optical fibres, she said: "You know, Marli understood that everything that we ever did was for the future."

"But she was *my* mother," I shot back from the entrance of her hut, as if it meant something. "And she's given up her life for something *you* believed in. No, Arisa, you *will* help me."

"What do you mean?"

"You *will* help me find out what happened to Ibu."

"But you already know what happened to her, child."

"I mean, *where*." Arisa stared at me. "You saw it," I said, my tone accusing her again. "She found ... a new species of seaweed, out there, in the midlight. And I need to know why it was so important to her – I need to know *where*."

"Why?"

*Why?* "You said it, didn't you? It's for the future, for science." *For me!*

"Rumi –"

"Besides," I said, cutting her off, "I know that you know exactly *where* she'd been."

Swiftly, Arisa's black eyes regained their sharp aspect. They were cold and calculated. Resolute. Good. I was unaccustomed to the emotional and empathetic side of Arisa.

Ten years earlier, she had come to our village and recruited Ibu with wads of cash, as if the Bajau had only dealt with barter. We were harnessing solar energy for our phones and tablets long before the Indonesian government offered us more stable livelihoods based on drone-enabled fishing and seaweed farming. For taking away our dying art of bare-handed pearl diving and fishing, it seemed we were meant to thank them.

But perhaps what neither Arisa nor the government truly understood about us was why we persisted in keeping our traditions of freediving and living free on the sea. As for us, we couldn't understand why both the government and Arisa spent so much time and so many resources to look for some rare, still-unknown species of marine life that could help decarbonise the atmosphere or oxygenate the seas, when what needed to be done to save the world should have been done long ago. Not now. Not here. Not in a hurry.

Staring at me, Arisa asked: "Hold on. How could you know I know something like that?"

"You must have found something, as you were so late to Ibu's funeral."

I saw Arisa sucking in her breath, and continued: "And you must have been curious about the seaweed, and about why and how Ibu had died."

Arisa sighed. "Oh, I don't know if the word for it is *curious*, child. But, yes, I might have detected Marli's wrist tracker using the equipment on my boat this morning."

"So you *did* find something."

"Look, I don't know if it's *something*," Arisa answered, sweeping an arm around her hut, pointing to everything. "And I don't know if it's something worth *pursuing*."

"Don't say that," I whispered, as Arisa fell silent. "Ibu didn't die over *nothing*."

Arisa nodded. "But Rumi, if we are to do this, we must do this *my* way, with *my* equipment."

"Why?"

"Listen, wherever Marli found herself in, it must've been dangerous. And if it had been so for Marli – for *your* mother – it will be doubly so for you. You can't deny this."

I didn't.

Arisa explained that Ibu had been investigating an area of continental shelf that hadn't yet been explored. We didn't think to; just east of the village, it was precariously close to an active volcanic island, Batutara, which had been spewing ash and triggering earthquakes for years. Its state was so volatile, it sometimes created dead zones in the surrounding sea, glutted with toxic algae and marred by lava flows. Carbon dioxide and sulphurous fumes were dissolved directly into the mid-light waters of these dead zones. There was no other reason except for Arisa's research that Ibu would venture there.

"Then all the more reason we shouldn't head there." Arisa was vacillating now, loudly but half-heartedly. She was drinking copious amounts of *sopi* as we sat with our legs dangling over the edge of her hut.

I studied the deep, feathered creases in her face, flushed red with warmth and illuminated by the yellow bioluminescent lamp in her hut. I smelled the cloying sweetness on her breath competing with the saltiness of the breeze around us. I wasn't sure if I felt closer to Arisa than I ordinarily did. I felt she had betrayed Ibu – and for what? Ambition?

"You're still a child; no, you're *her* child."

"I'm not a child anymore, Arisa. I'm nearly sixteen."

"Not nearly sixteen at all, Rumi. Not even close."

At dawn, Arisa and I were at least equally determined to set off for Batutara.

As she started up the engine of her boat, fiddling with the latest maritime and scientific paraphernalia, I sat on its solar roof and watched the dark sky lightening to dusty blue from the stern. For a few minutes, all I did was watch the crepuscular rays of the rising sun scatter against the low-lying clouds, painting them in streaks of rosy pink. I took in the crisp morning air with the smell of brine and relished in the sea winds brushing against my darkened, sun-parched skin.

When we were far enough away, I turned to look back at the village. Square-hewn seaweed farms by the hundreds demarcated its shoreline. Each square was occupied by a tube-shaped, solar-powered drone scooping up the rope-grown seaweed and laying it down in the water again after trimming it perfectly. The village farmers still had to remove invasive seagrasses or sea urchins by hand to protect their aquatic crop, so a few of them were already up and about as we headed east into the open sea.

As the seaweed farms shrank in the distance, the village's free-floating fish farms came up in the horizon. Looking at them from above, they appeared as grey geodesic domes. To ensure that the free-range fish being reared inside these massive, seemingly self-sufficient spherical farms were safe to eat, numerous divers checked on them daily. Marine drones supported their work, helping to harvest the fish and alert them to any openings made by sharks or thieves. But anything else that required a subtle touch still had to be done by a professional diver, which is what Ibu and I could have become, but didn't.

Once we travelled past the fish farms, we hardly met other boats or man-made structures. Only once were we interrupted by a pod of dolphins, breaching in the frothy playground of the boat's wake and playing catch with a piece of kelp in their snouts. Their tittering attracted Arisa's attention. She came out to the stern and took videos of them.

"They're a good sign, aren't they?" she shouted

up at me, but I waved her off. *It is not she who will be risking her life looking for some mystical seaweed.*

Before I was prepared for it, we soon arrived on the jade green shores of Batutara. On seeing the volcano up close, coughing plumes of ash and smoke into the dark, grainy clouds above it, fear crept up in me. Worse, the more time I spent on the boat with Arisa, who was refreshing my memory of how to use a mask, a pair of fins, a rebreather and even the white wetsuit she had prepared for me, the more scared I felt. It started innocently enough, as mild tremors in my fingers and toes, but grew to a spine-rattling chill that felt as though it extended right down to my groin.

"Are you listening to me, child?" I wasn't. I was too aware of my heartbeat pounding in my temples and my throat tightening in dread than anything else. "I need to tell you something before you go into the water." I didn't respond. I was trying my hardest to conceal my fear, and failing. "Marli never wished this life for you."

"I know."

"Yes, so ... Couldn't you say that you chose this life for yourself, Rumi?" Arisa's face was so close to mine, I could see the flakes of dry skin around the edges of her mouth and along her silvery white hairline. I didn't want to trust anything more she said, but on this wide expanse of ocean, above the place where Ibu was last alive, she was my only friend. "You must know: even though your mother was the more experienced freediver, you are her better. She always said that you were faster. Smarter. And that you can hold your breath for longer. I didn't know why Marli wanted to stop you from becoming a freediver, but to me, you are her natural successor. Her future."

Although it didn't sound like Ibu at all, I wanted to believe Arisa. I wanted to feel that when I finally stepped into the ocean, it would be an adventure, not an obligation to either Arisa or Ibu, or a mere reckless endeavour.

At the very least, its warm, wet embrace felt familiar. Its cavernous silence in my ears soothed and composed me, while I became more accustomed to its enveloping pressure around my head, my chest. Stretching to my full length, I used my arms and legs to start my descent.

*Drop. Kick. Glide. Stroke.*

Four steps were all Ibu had needed to teach me about freediving. Forget about breathing or being human. And as I reached the depths of the ocean, aided but not reliant on Arisa's rebreather, I etched those four steps deep into the recesses of my mind.

The first thing I noticed about the waters surrounding Batutara was the mist.

I wasn't sure if it was from the gases released by some undersea magma, or from the coral spawn of such a crowded, multifaceted reef. But while I saw countless species of fish, crustacean and algae, there was nothing like what Ibu had found. I swam leisurely and patiently along the rocky and uneven shelf of sea, until inspiration struck me.

*Wait – what if the seaweed Ibu had found had both green and red algae characteristics? It was a new species, wasn't it? What if it could control whether it photosynthesises in sunlight or blue light?*

In an instant, I looked for a drop in the ocean – a crack, a fissure – or any shaded and obscured area where sunlight could penetrate, but only teasingly. Gradually, I did manage to notice a glimmer pricking the corner of my eye through Arisa's mask, and headed straight for it. I thought it was a sign from Ibu. A clue. When I discovered it was a just a small, transparent section of plastic, my hopes deflated.

In its former life, it might have been important. It could have been a protective cover for food or medicine. But down here, it was fodder for whales and bottom feeders. Fodder for bacteria and ... and *algae*.

Following the trail of plastic, I went further along the shelf to a place where the coral reef hadn't yet been colonised, and came across a gushing underwater river teeming with plastic. The sheer amount of plastic in between these layers of dark, maroon-hued rock caused it to scintillate when sunlight bounced off it, like a stream of aquamarines. I imagined a kind of undertow had formed to compensate for the waves approaching Batutara's shoreline, which then drew in all this plastic and trash and even marine life straight down into this river.

It looked as though, over time, a strange kind of sea habitat had developed inside it, thrived inside it. But as the opening of the river was so constricted and shallow, I knew I would have to leave behind all of Arisa's diving equipment just to explore it.

I looked across to the jutted riverbank, seeking more signs that Ibu could have been here, but didn't need to search far – her solar-powered wrist tracker was sitting just on top of it. Upon my picking it up, it died. But with its final flash in muted white and blue, it told me that it had, at least, communicated with Arisa's boat. And in this, I supposed, for me, it marked my point of no return.

I took the deepest drag of breath I had taken in sixteen years and abandoned everything that Arisa had given me to drop down to the bottom of the underwater river. At this depth of about seventy metres from the surface, it almost felt like I was flying – like I was airborne in the sea. It made me forget that my chest was collapsing, and every inch of my body was being pummelled by pressure, which caused me to *drop, drop, drop* into the belly of the reef.

I didn't fight it.

I felt it flow over me, gently pushing me to walk along the riverbed of plastic, as I continued to find the next clue that Ibu had seen. I must have looked for barely a few minutes, but every minute in these harsh, cold depths felt like eternity.

I couldn't explain it.

Arisa would say it was science that guided me to another fissure, another crack on the ocean floor, but I would like to think that it was Nyai Lara's whispers: *What do you think you're doing here? Didn't I already warn off your mother, who dared to make off with something that belongs to me? How dare you presume to visit my undersea river, my undersea cavern dwelling – you and your mother! Come here, you, I'll show you. I'll show you.*

I knew I had passed the hundred-metre mark when I started suffocating, and felt an excruciating pain pulsing through my head, chest and gut. All around me, there was only darkness, and the sensation of rocks underneath my hands and feet. Before, I had believed I was flying. Now, I was crawling on my knees, and begging and praying to Nyai Lara to spare me, to save me. I knew that in these most gruelling moments, in this most testing environment, Ibu had found a means to live. But my hands were growing heavy and paralysed. My legs were freezing over. My lungs, oh ... forget my lungs ...

The only thing that was still stirring with activity was my mind. My mind was still alive. And not even Nyai Lara could take it away from me.

When my lungs came back to life, euphoria swept over me. I couldn't have cared less that I might be breathing water instead of air. I gulped down litres of it, ravenously, through my mouth and felt my chest swiftly expanding. With my eyes adjusting to the dimness, I saw that I had ended up in an air pocket inside a tight, confined space enclosed within columns of rock. I struggled to recall what had happened after I had dived into the underwater river. I thought I must have climbed into an underwater tunnel of sorts, which had led me here – but how?

*I must have died,* I thought. How else could I explain the oxygen here, in this cave more than a hundred metres below where the sea met the sky?

Looking closer at the rough, rocky walls around me, focusing my eyes on them and touching them, I realised that they were not just made of rock, but were also covered in seaweed – Ibu's seaweed. I laughed when I spotted it – a spluttering cough. I allowed its soft, silky texture to soothe me as I ran my fingers through its impressive, moss-green carpet, and regarded with reverence its scarlet veins running through its almost-translucent fronds.

Like mine, its veins were pumping essential nutrients and gases, helping it to stay alive. Except, unlike me, it was breathing in carbon dioxide and releasing oxygen. *Now, wait a second – oxygen?* How could just a few seaweeds produce so much oxygen that they would create an air pocket at the bottom of the ocean?

As Ibu's body had been washed ashore on the

beach just outside the village, I knew she had made it out of this cave alive. She had managed to use her knowledge of the currents and tides to swim, perhaps, halfway to the village before she drowned. Yet she didn't risk her life to bring this seaweed back to Arisa, or for Arisa's research. No. Ibu must have risked everything to bring it back to *me*.

It was me. I did this.

After all those years with Arisa, Ibu knew that this seaweed – no, this *discovery* – was not just life-changing, but world-changing. I could see from the seaweed that was barely submerged that it was not just pearling, but nearly effervescing with oxygenated air. And manufacturing it at numerous times the rate of nothing I had ever seen.

Without bringing any of the seaweed with me, I made my way back to the ocean surface slowly and unhurriedly. Why shouldn't I? I knew the steps. I knew the path that Ibu had set out for me, even though it will be me who will become the final freediver on Earth.

*Stroke. Glide. Kick. Rise.*

Where I emerged was nowhere near Batutara or the village. I noticed that my own wrist tracker, too, had died.

Despite the ringing in my ears, I heard dolphins in the distance tempting me to follow them. I spared no time thinking about my lacerated lungs or salt-burned eyes, and thought only to do everything I had to, for as long as I had to, to protect Ibu's discovery.

# A HAT FOR LEMER

## CECIL BROWNE

*August 1858. St Vincent.*

Rain pelt the whole night in the mountains. It silence the animals that love to break my sleep, it join the wind and lash my tiny wooden shack where the volcano ridge break for a bit of flat. Next morning the sun battle back so fierce the storm seem like a bad dream. After such a stormy night, the ground still slippery, strange to spot someone struggling up the slope to my home as I'm coconut-oiling my hair. Caribs and runaways hunting wild pigs I could understand ... but a white man? And alone so deep in the mountains?

From the narrow slit of a window I catch the figure sweeping back the bushes like a paddler in a canoe. A heavy man with a red bulging food face. Mud splatter his trousers up to the belt, and the green jacket holding back his stomach catch a caking too. This man brave, what could he want with me? I slip out the back door and take a path through the forest. Sometimes, best to greet an intruder hugging a tree.

He make to take a step forward, his eyes on the house as if it might disappear if he look away. Before he could tell himself *Not far to go*, he fall flat on his back.

"Fucking Satan."

He stagger to his feet, furious with some dry stick he didn't notice in his path. When he finish brushing off his clothes he find me beside him, my narrow face soft but closed to him.

"You tripped me," he growl, "you frigging throw me down!"

The blue veins in his neck pulse, this local-born Creole white who blend our language with his. But I don't step back when he snarl and grunt. He on Crown land, *my* land. I cross my arms and stare back.

"My name is Noah Brisbane," he say after a while. "My horseman Mel tell me you know the island well. You guide people across the mountains and find those who get lost for a small sum." I dig my toes into the mud and force my body up the hill to my little garden patch, leaving him there muttering. Wheezing turn to cursing as he stumble up behind me. I almost finish picking herbs at the side of the house by the time he reach. "I own the estate nine miles from Kingstown capital."

Nine miles south of Kingstown would place him in the Caribbean Sea, nine north in Mespo Valley. West would find the town of Layou, where Reverend Alexander ship in his two hundred slaves from Antigua because he care for them so much. The Brisbane now squatting on a stone in my yard must mean east, then, the Diamond Estate. I begin to pack a crocus bag with herbs while he sweep the sweat from his forehead. My work is in listening: I ask when I'm ready.

Brisbane take my silence to mean that I curious, so he say, "You want to know why I'm here, I suppose?"

I don't answer him. My herbs are my living.

"Well, two weeks ago I invited an Englishman

to my home. Wesley String. The Methodist Church in England sent him to St Vincent to report on the schools, but he's vanished.

*"Schools?"* Brisbane ask the question for me, then continue. "You remember emancipation in 1838? Well schools spring up on coconut-palm stilts. And where schools rise, inspectors follow."

Fuck Brisbane. Emancipation handed some planters thousands of pounds. If February slip by without a fete, then March pay with three.

"How long he here?"

"One month." I sniff a bundle of thyme and let Brisbane carry on. "I put on a small feast for String. Beef, red snapper, ham, breadfruit, bananas. We have to show our guests the best of the island, not true? My cook Eva did us proud. I pay her an extra shilling."

Brisbane flip his head back a little as his eyes close on the memory of the meal. "A chill hit us late in the evening, so I sent for a brandy. My wife Georgina changed into her green silk dress and String drained his glass. 'Another tiddly bottle?' he suggested. 'Hats off to a new friendship, eh Brisbane?'"

Creole-white life not our life, but Brisbane too sweet in his memories to care. "String took his breakfast early on the Monday so he could go and inspect a school. He show me his schedule, another one on Thursday. 'Then join us for the Governor's dinner up Fort Charlotte,' I suggest to him. 'Seven o'clock sharp.' But he never arrive. I had my men out looking five days, but no good."

I was ready to talk for myself. "You try the taverns in Kingstown?" I say. "They tell me some men can't down their rum unless women serve them."

"Not String. He rarely touched liquor – he swore to my wife when she was showing him to his bedroom chamber."

"Religious men toss their Bible overboard in the middle of the Atlantic."

"Some perhaps, but not String."

"What you think happened to him?"

"If I believed in spirits, I would say an evil one bundled him away to Dominica. I just pray no harm come to him."

"Harm?"

"Caribs don't take to people on their land.

Trespassing or plain lost, no difference. Every white is a British soldier; they don't spare the poison arrow."

"How much you paying to find him?"

"Two pounds."

Magistrate Anderson earn £32 a month – I read this in the *Gazette* newspaper – so I tell Brisbane: "Eight. Or send your cook to search for him."

"I can't raise above three."

"Then particular on your way down the volcano."

"*Eight*, you said? Call it seven, then." Seven pounds still need two hands to count, so I nod. "Work fast," Brisbane say. "String vessel leaving in a month; we have to find him so he can fulfil his mission."

"Which school he visit?"

"Stubbs, two rivers away."

"The teacher?"

"The Grimbles, ginger-haired mulatto brother and sister."

Brisbane describe String to me as I guide him back down: tall, bald, love a felt hat. Three men waiting for Brisbane at the base of the volcano, and four black horses that could pass for brown. Clothes and animals all caked with mud: earth don't separate black and white. As they about to ride off, Brisbane say, "Send me news soon as you locate String." But not before his horseman Mel fix me a look that say: *Come find me.*

One missing Englishman. Brisbane trek through thick bamboo forest and sharp cane leaves for the sake of one white man! On every barracks he cross lame chigger-foot children and men who work their body down to the bones and shrink back to boys. Women groan in agony when they shift from raw stomachs onto sore backs. But Brisbane willing to ride through hellhole estates, where the stinking breeze make you want to faint, all because of some blasted inspector?

When I think of the hole my family escape I thank the mother, who encourage my father. He lead the family off the Soleyn property when I turn twelve. One dark damp night that drive the workers into the barracks shared with heat and stubborn flies, we steal away and head north toward the volcano. We stumble and we slip. We shelter under trees high and low. Whole night we journey, till the sharp stones of the river bed tell us we arrive.

Even the trackers with their hound dogs fear this tangle mountain forest. Creaking, ghost-like bamboo trees and squawking animals scare them away, and the stink of volcano sulphur in the air protect us. We settle into a thin life, creeping by some estate at night to barter and to sing with the people, then crawling home in darkness, or humming under a kindly moonlight.

What Brisbane know about me? That I live on fruits, vegetables, the wild pigs and agouti we trap, and the crayfish and mullets that cram the nearby streams? That the Lomond family I guide to a mountain home race back to the comfort of flies, cockroaches and mangy dogs that infest the Punnett estate? That on rainy nights I peep out my wooden shack and long for someone to see out the storm with?

Farthings, shillings, pretty pound notes. I see them at the market exchanging for sugar, for fruits, for meat. Shillings I handle, but my fingers never brush a pound note. A house, a bed, three chairs, maybe four. A coal pot, plates, enamel cups. Seven pounds could build *two* good-size houses. But where to begin to search for some man with a stupid name?

I close my eyes, thank the Moravians who teach me to read, write and reckon, and pray like a child who rather die than separate from her mother.

• • •

No good starting this mystery in the capital, my feet tell me when I set out at dawn next morning. String probably blind-drunk in some gutter there. Sailors and corporals grab a bottle soon as they dock, three comforts satisfy men. If not, String lodging with some grateful woman, clothing her children and providing corned pork and bread for their supper. The Grimbles see him last, but Mel send me a sign. Which one to visit first?

Sun roasting my four thick plaits, it take me the whole morning to walk to Stubbs. My soles accustom to distance, but they ache, and the rest of my body join in. I spot the teacher directly I enter the schoolyard: a meagre man in a green suit squatting under a hog-plum tree, crunching peanuts.

"You here to enrol a child?" he ask. The sea close by. I watch the waves roll up to the black sand, froth, then race back to the big blue. Brother Grimble rise and wipe his mouth. "Best school in the parish. A Englishman come here trying to tell *me* how to teach children. Some woman nibble his neck, he should thank God I didn't bust his red lip for balance."

Thirty pupils on the school register that Grimble draw from his pocket to show me. I spot two sleeping under a cedar tree and five on the beach flinging stones, taunting the sea. The Moravians placed the *Gazette* newspaper alongside the Bible to teach us when I was a girl; now, twenty years later, Grimble ask me to watch the pupils dance. He call a girl in a blue tunic with two fat plaits sticking out a brown felt hat.

"June September," he say, "the best on the island."

I watch.

"Show the woman how you dance for the Inspector." June shake her head. "Dance!"

"No, Mr Grimble."

"Dance, I say!"

I tap Grimble on the shoulder and give him a gentle smile: "Leave her."

Grimble stuff the register in his pocket and tighten his body like he intend to cuff me. His mule catch his mood and start pissing in the bushes nearby. Grimble mount the pissing mule and ride away. I wait for the children to set off home, then begin trailing him to Vigie. And is only then June pretty tunic and felt hat cause me to consider.

Creoles and whites own horses; for those who can't afford higher animals, a mule, donkey or footing the road is your pleasure. I limp back home from Vigie and sit by a cool stream, soaking my feet. Later, squatting on my dirt floor, I pick at my smoked herring and bread supper. Further up the volcano, my parents have their own rude home. I visit them to check they ride out the storm.

My grey-haired father fall silent soon as I arrive. He still aggrieved since I reject a tailor suitor from Adelphi he bring to my home. He barely lift his eyes to greet me now. I tell them about Brisbane. When I mention the amount my mother pause twisting her hair, turn to the four corners of the hut and imagine a house ten times the size.

"Lemer," my father mumble when I leaving, "Brisbane want to rise in the Methodist Church. Careful."

Back in my house, Mel come to my mind as I fix the old sheet round my body to block the night chill. What message he could have for me? I slip onto Brisbane estate next day to find out.

The women crossing me wearing coarse dresses that have more dust and holes than cloth, so I fit in easy. I seek out a short coconut tree leaning to the left that could take the curl of my weary back. From this tree on the bank of Diamond River I watch Mel grooming his horse. My cinnamon smell probably drift to him, because after a little while, he cry out:

"Lemer!" A brown felt hat sit high on Mel

broad head, then he naked down to the waist. "You watching me long?"

I approach the horse and stroke it. "No."

"She beautiful, not true?"

"She have a kind face."

"'Black Belle' she name, but I call she 'Pretty Eva'."

"Like Brisbane cook?"

"*Old* cook."

"How you mean?"

"Eva walk off Diamond."

"When? Why she leave?"

"Three days after String come to the house. Brisbane does French she when she take his breakfast, and pay she five shillings a time."

*"French?"*

"Yes French. See Black Belle here, Brisbane present she to me. Why? To lock the door when he Frenching. I don't know what happen between she, String and Brisbane, but whole day Eva anxious. She take thirty pounds from Brisbane money chest and Wednesday night, gone she gone."

Some women heading their bundle of washing

take the turning for the river just then; I duck into the bushes so they don't see the horseman talking to me. So early into my journey, yet I already feel sorry I sell my peace.

But whether for shillings or pounds, a task is a task. So the next day, on the mule I borrow from my mother, I ride to String's house in Lowmans. The front door lock, so I climb through a window. A Bible on his desk. Seven felt hats dot the bed. A trunk sit in a corner, but the three locks too tough for my fingers. If String join a bunch of sailors roaming the island while he prepare his report, wouldn't surprise me.

From Lowmans I ride direct to the market in Kingstown. People from every town or village trade there. Tomatoes, bananas, yams and mangoes aplenty, fowls, pigs and goats mingle. Reach for a fat pumpkin and don't surprise if you catch a frisky land crab. Let a white go missing or die, and the news usually flood the market. Like whites don't die, they live forever! I don't stay long at the market, though, the breeze bring no mention of String. And where I used to see codfish, plums or sheets, now pretty cotton dresses, shingle, nails and lumber winking at me.

Kingstown a most pretty town. The market and a dozen shops flavour the capital. On Saturdays you can't move for horses, carts, mules and donkeys in the narrow streets. One distiller family I guide across the island for two shillings call the town *food, liquor, fete and flesh*. Four parlour taverns line Bay Street, ugly wooden shacks that lean left or right like they dodging the midday sun. In the dirt yard of the first three, rum-soaked men curl up on their side. Their lips red and raw, even flies shun them. The last parlour – Whisper – brick upstairs and downstairs. This would be the place for a foreigner.

Our family trek to the market every week to sell herbs, and field hands, cane cutters, midwives, seamstresses, coopers and messengers make the trip to Kingstown on pay day. Most go for the goods at the market; the rest head direct to the parlours. But a place like Whisper strange to me. The people who rest up there wild, so I hear.

I sit on the cobblestones watching the door, my body tense like the morning I wake and find a snake coil up next to my naked breast. Nights in the mountains don't trouble me, but this place? As I watch women enter and men stumble out and stagger away, I make the sign of the cross. Lord help and forgive me. I wait till four women shouldering their market baskets squeeze through the door and add one to their number.

Noise hit me, right behind the sweet smell of hot food. Whiskey and rum thicken the cigar smoke. Two men in white strumming *cuatros* in a corner, soldiers and sailors singing merrily along. Women from the estates in their best clothes parading with soldiers, hugging up so tight like they twine. Parlour women dancing in the middle of the room. Which angel teach them such pretty steps? In long frilly dresses, every hue of black and every shade of white parcel out between them. My coarse brown osnaburg dress just one stitch up from rags, I stare at the women in admiration, in shame.

"What you want?"

I turn to my right to see who touch me on the shoulder. I find a woman, same age and blackness, with a fragrant smell of ripe cocoa to my sweaty cinnamon. The woman's purple dress flow down to her ankles. I make to answer, but her almond-shape eyes so bewitching she lock the words in my throat.

"If you looking to join Whisper, sorry."

I shake my head quick.

"You searching for somebody, then?"

"A white man, Wesley String."

"He tell you to meet him here?"

"No."

"What, then?"

"I just have to find him. And quick."

"You sound like a country Mary. Outside cooler, follow me."

Out in the light, the woman lower herself on a log and fold her dress between her thighs.

"Your white man," she say. "You making his baby?"

"No. This estate owner pay me to find him."

"How he describe?"

"Tall underneath a felt hat."

"Good heap of sizeable men frolic here. Once a ship dock, the women can't rest."

"This man resemble a schoolmaster."

The woman consider. "And twin with a fat man?"

Brisbane large, String heighten, so I nod. "Maybe."

"Those two revel here. Brandy upon whiskey. But the girls couldn't get a task out of them. Woman-food too rich for some."

"They stay late?"

"Nah. A fresh set of men storm Whisper at dusk, and the teacher and the whale dive deep!"

"Why?"

"Men only duck when they have something to hide."

I don't know what make me do it, but I stoop and stretch for the woman's hands. They soft and warm. I pray my trembling fingers don't tell her is the first time I touch another person like this.

She let her fingers rest in mine. I have to stop myself caressing them.

"Stop by Grenville Street after you find your husband, String," she say. "Ask for Whisper."

"You own the tavern?"

"Yes, country Mary."

• • •

A fever grip me that night. Then a chill. I wrap the sheet around my body, and I feel like my skin roasting. When I peel off the sheet, I begin to shiver. My body like it leaving me behind.

The dawn two days later, hugging a guava tree, I watching Brisbane. Most estates have a Big House; some have a Little House too, away from the mansion. Brisbane by his Little House admiring the sea. From Mel's tale he work on his accounts early, then take his breakfast when the figures balance. More than a fortnight Georgina away visiting her sister – Mel laugh – which woman would leave her husband when he in agony over his friend?

When Brisbane over with the sea, he slip into the building and close the door. No Eva this morning. No removing the frilly cotton frock and watching it wriggle to the floor. No closing his eyes in delight while he undo the black drawers that frenzy him. No Frenching.

As Brisbane make to sit before the account book, he feel the give of my thigh. He spring back up.

"Lemer!" he cry. "How did you get in?"

I don't answer. I watch his neck spin, searching for some door or window I smash to get in.

"Who told you I was here?"

Same no answer.

"Never mind," Brisbane mumble, "long as you don't swallow the blasted lies my workers spread."

"I know about you and String," I say now.

"You found him?"

"No."

"What, then?"

"You write your own commandments."

"You talking in riddles. I'm not paying you seven pounds to break into my house and make accusations."

"*Whisper*, Brisbane," I say to him. "You know the inn on Bay Street?"

"I know the street. The inn, no."

"So wasn't you staggering out at dusk behind a hatted man couple weeks ago?"

"Bring the person who told you that tale and I'll show you a blasted liar."

I watch Brisbane good. The white in his face steadfast. No dip to pale, no flushing crimson. Who to believe, this estate owner or angel Whisper?

"*Ecclesiastes* 3, Brisbane," I warn him. "You know the verse?"

He grin. "Remind me."

*"Everything in its season."*

Brisbane open the drawer and grab a handful of coins. He spread them clinking on the table in front me. "Get out of my chair and leave my property!"

My left hand stop my right from making a fist.

"I'll call my men!"

"If you or your men touch me," I say, "make sure you don't sleep tonight."

The door creak open, and a child in a purple tunic and a brown felt hat appear with a tray.

"Is me, Mr Brisbane. I bring your breakfast. And I bathe in the river like you tell me."

Brisbane rush over, take the girl by the shoulder and guide her out.

"Carry the tray back to the Big House, June. I'm taking my breakfast there today."

June hurry off. Soon as the child leave, I turn to Brisbane. "Twice seven is fourteen," I say.

"Don't set foot on my property again unless you have String with you!"

• • •

It rain from sunrise to sunset next day, so I sleep off my vexation. My head hot. I pray for matches to burn down Brisbane Little House. Fever grip my body. I lie on my back on the floor listening to the rain pelting, falling asleep, waking, then falling asleep again. In between sleep and wake, Whisper come to me, smiling. *"Come join the angels, Lemer."*

When the fever through with me I set off for Vigie again, on foot. Brother Grimble have a grudge against String. Wonder if he more than want to bust his lip?

A ginger-haired woman with a felt hat over her face snoozing on a stone in the backyard. She wake quick-quick when she hear my footsteps.

"Five tens make sixty," she say. "You have a child to register?"

"No," I say, "I looking for String."

Sister Grimble frown. "You in Vigie School, Miss, not some cheap semi-demi shop. No string here."

Brother Grimble appear from behind a fat *mapu* tree trunk as if he was hiding there.

"If String set foot in Stubbs or Vigie School again," he warn, "he spend his last day on Earth."

"He proposition me," Sister Grimble say. "Then he present me this hat when I threaten to report him. *Inspector*, my ginger-mulatto batty."

• • •

Is a long journey to the docks in Kingstown. On the way I think hard about what the Grimbles say about the Englishman. I think about Eva, Georgina, Brisbane – and two houses. People crowding me, wild dreams, felt hats. My head all tangle up.

The docks frenzying when I get there. Carts, porters, messengers, sailors and passengers scrambling like ants to a dead-butterfly banquet. I sit on the beach, admiring the blue-green sea and wondering what lie beyond. When my mind settled, I approach the port office.

The clerk of good height. He come at me with pretty white teeth.

"The passenger lists," I say to him. "How much to see them?"

"A guinea."

"Hefty amount."

"Looking cost. Which day you after?"

"The last fortnight."

"You too?"

"Someone else pay to see them?"

"Some estate horseman. He sit on the dock every day and watch which vessel leaving the island."

"I only have a shilling."

The clerk smile. "Come closer and try for a better price."

I stand same place and cross my arms. He approach and circle me three times like he weaving a spell.

"Cinnamon," he say, bigging his eyes. "Pay me the rest in that smell."

I close my eyes. And sigh.

My father's words come back to me as I make for Grenville Street. Brisbane have his horseman looking too; what String have that could damage him?

The road to Whisper place have cobblestones in a pretty pattern. Whisper abode upstairs in a brick house. I shout out her name. Before I could call back the word, back-back and run away, the door open.

My skin is there to cover my bones. Whisper body have a softness and shape that make me shy away as she prepare for the parlour tavern. The room fragrant, as if she gather the best spices on the island. I sit forward on a chair and watch her dress, slow, so slow. Then I can't help myself, I reach over and take her breasts. They full, like ripe mangoes. I want to plant my teeth into them until she burst. But Whisper place her hands over mine and quiver soft: "No, Lemer ... no."

I try to ease my hands away but she lock hers on top mine: "No."

I spend the afternoon. Whisper gift me four pretty dresses and some shoes. I bathe, try on the dresses and feel – first time – the brush of proper cloth against my skin. Lucky me.

On the way to the parlour in the dusk, lucky me again, Whisper stop suddenly by a semi-demi shop. Chairs, ale, chickens, fruits, vegetables, wines, yams, figs and spices selling, everything everywhere. In a little space in a corner the owner squatting stuffing bread, ham, porter, eggs, cheese and saltfish into a basket. His head shiny black.

"*Mesdames?*" he say, "I'm Jean-Pierre, from Martinique. What is your pleasure today?"

"The sheets." Whisper point to a heap on a chair. "How much?"

As Jean-Pierre rubbing his chin to come up with a figure, I spot a dozen brown felt hats pile up on a box.

"The hats from Martinique too?"

"No, London."

"How much for one?"

"*Monsieur* String sell me for four, but for you pretty ladies, three."

"String?"

"An Englishman. I'm just preparing him a leaving basket."

"He leaving St Vincent?"

"Yes. He catching a boat up north."

That same night, I do a shameful thing. So many felt hats on String bed, so many people spruce in one, I have to have one too, before String leave. And for free. But when I break into the house, not a single hat there! I smash open the trunk with a big stone, and what scatter out more than felt hats? And in a Bible at the bottom of the trunk, what staring me in the face if not £45? HARRIS BIGGA, LONDON, the side of the trunk marked.

• • •

When dusk coming on next day, I tracking Jean-Pierre. He carrying two heavy baskets on his horse. A house deep in Jennings Valley is where he lead me. What business he have in thick mountains this late?

Two people step out into the dirt yard when they hear the horse trotting. Even in the darkness, I make them out: a tall man under a felt hat, and a woman. The woman carry one basket inside, the man grab the other.

"Harris Bigga!" I shout in the darkness.

The man head turn, so I step forward to greet the runaways. And to ask the price of the hats he selling.

Two journeys more, and my task over. I cross the mountains under a kind Friday moonlight; by morning I arrive in Chateaubelair town. Women and children bathing in the sea, a few fishermen tossing line, none of the talk I expect to hear about a sailing. So is a second trip over the volcano that night to Owia on the windward coast.

My weary body flop down on the beach. I could sleep for a week. Voices wake me before sleep call me home proper. I scramble up and find a fifty-foot Carib canoe about to launch. And in among the Caribs I spot String offering his hand to a pretty woman in a purple dress. Brisbane and Mel watching the launch, too. They get my message, soon I can rest my head.

"String!" Brisbane yell as the passengers settle. "Eva!"

"I'm off to St Lucia, Brisbane!" String shout back. "To finish my report."

"You can't leave! What about the £100 I loaned you?"

"Someone broke into my home and stole half of it. I gave the rest to Georgina. Thanks for the excellent treatment I had in the Big House."

"You saw Georgina?"

"Sorry, Brisbane, we have to leave to avoid the midday sun. My report will give you a glorious mention."

Eva sit, then give a gentle wave: "Goodbye Mr Brisbane."

The Caribs reach for the oars, and soon all we can see is a speck in the distance.

"The thief! The drunkard, the rogue! I want my money back." Brisbane face swell with anger. "He can write that the Devil is blue, in his report!"

"Forget String," I tell Brisbane, "no report coming."

"But he was sent to inspect the schools!"

"No, Brisbane. String is a hat seller. And what he can't sell, he look for payment some another way."

"So my £100 is gone?"

"Yes. All the time you pretending you hope String safe from the Caribs, was the money that concern you."

"But he swore he was a Methodist."

"An inspector who finish your brandy, stagger out the Whisper parlour in Kingstown, only visit two schools. Wish Eva good luck with him."

Brisbane look away and say soft, *"Eva."*

"Eva gone, Brisbane."

He turn to face me. Is a struggle to keep his head level with mine. "Come to Diamond tomorrow for your fee. Seven pounds?"

I don't have to think about it.

"Give it to June parents to build a house."

# BRIDGE OVER THE YALLAHS RIVER

## DIANA MCCAULAY

*When since thunderstorm mean disaster?* thought Roy. He waited to count the seconds between lightning and thunder, assessing how far away the storm was. Rain pounded on the zinc roof. Flash, flash; then a rolling boom that travelled from sky to earth, and shook his bed. *Six seconds. Not that close.*

He couldn't hear his daughter's breathing, so he bent over her, feeling her breath feathering his cheek. A storm could cause her to have an asthma attack, and the roads were probably already impassable.

Deena began to wheeze. "Sit up, punkin," Roy said, pulling her into his arms. "Where you inhaler?" Deena reached under her pillow, her eyes unfocused. She shook the inhaler and it rattled. She breathed out and then sucked at it.

Roy stroked her hair. "Jus breathe. Storm soon pass." Flash, crash. Eight seconds. Then they heard a mechanical, tearing, screeching sound over the rain. "Must be di bridge," whispered Roy, more to himself than to Deena. *Disaster had a shape and a date,* he thought. He could just see Deena's chest rise, hitch and fall in the dark. How long would the stuff in the inhaler last? Their house was higher than some, but how would he know if the river had burst its banks and they had to climb onto the roof?

The rain eased just after dawn. He left Deena sleeping and went outside into a drizzle. The Yallahs River was still a raging, roiling scar across the land. He had built his house on a slight slope and used concrete foundations to raise the floor – it had never flooded. Not yet. He jumped onto a crumbling wall nearby – part of an old aqueduct, the elders said – and stood looking east over the community of Back To toward the river. In the glow of dawn, he saw the bridge was really gone.

Every resident of Back To knew the story

of the bridge, first built in slavery time. It had been cracked by an earthquake at the turn of the twentieth century. Later that same year, a huge guango tree had been washed down by the rains and trapped by the bridge itself, backing up the silt-laden floodwaters which then spread across the land. Public Works blew up the bridge, because it was easier than taking out the tree. A new bridge was built, erected in less than a month by shirtless Black men supervised by sunburned white men wearing hard hats and orange vests. A "bailey" bridge, it was called, the elders said – a wondrous contraption of steel triangles and wooden planks, much higher over the river than the old one. The bailey bridge was supposed to be temporary, but the people of Back To thought it would be there forever, so modern and clean it was. And it did last for nearly seventy years – but slowly, the riverbanks began to erode, caused by sand miners and loggers in the mountains and recurrent floods, and soon there was a trench across the road near to the posts that supported the bridge. "Soon be bridge to no damn place," the people of Back To muttered.

Now the bridge was gone. No one would be able to cross the churning river for days until its waters subsided. There was a fording nearby, usable most of the year, because the Yallahs River had been diverted to the city of Kingston until only a trickle was left.

Roy jumped down from the wall to see to his daughter's tea. The Back To All-Age School was on the other side of the river, so there would be no school today.

Two days later, the politicians and Works agency people from Kingston and the bosses from the limestone quarry above Back To came to see the river-without-a-bridge. They shook their heads and shouted into their phones. Roy and Jonesy watched them from a safe distance. Maybe there would be work. But the water level fell day after day, and soon even one of the small Mazdas could use the fording. People began to cross on foot. Work at the quarry stopped, and the politicians and government people did not return.

"Fuckers," said Jonesy. "Dem don't give one shit 'bout di likes of wi."

Four months after Public Works blew up the bailey bridge and it washed into the sea, where it remained – a resting place for seabirds – Roy heard that the bridge was going to be rebuilt so the quarry could open.

He went looking for Jonesy.

"Look like dem hirin for di new bridge," Roy said, from the door of the RenkanFacety Bar.

Jonesy looked over his shoulder. "So mi hear. But is foreigner going build it. Chiney or Mexican." He turned back to his Red Stripe.

"Going give it a try, still. No steady work since last time dem fix it."

"If is Chiney-people, mi hear sey dem work you hard and pay you small."

Roy laughed. "Jonesy. What work you ever do dat not hard and pay small? Is work. Argument done."

Jonesy grunted. "Dem wait too late. Foolishness to start build before di hurricane season."

"You comin or not?"

"Can't hurt," Jonesy said, draining his beer.

They had been friends since childhood, both

born in Back To, a community of chaka-chaka zinc roof and plywood houses, solid concrete homes in government schemes, cookshops, rum bars, the All-Age school, a Methodist church, an Anglican church and the Church of the Living Ascension, set on a narrow plain between the mountains and the sea. The riverbed meandered over the plain, straightened and reinforced by gabion baskets in places, between crumbling banks in others, more sandy pathway than river most of the time.

Jonesy had recently returned after two years with his grandmother in Country – something to do with a fuss with a fisherman. Roy had never asked his friend about it. Their boyhood pact was to kick a football around the dusty playfield built by the quarry company, to look for rare river pools higher up that might still contain fish, to pick and sell red-coat plums and naseberries and stringy mangoes ... but never to fass in each other's business. The pact had held.

"Where dem hirin?" Jonesy asked as they walked. He smelled of beer and weed. It was not yet ten o'clock. He staggered a little, and Roy steadied him.

"Community centre. You go change you shirt? Put on a hat?" *Have a bath,* he wanted to say, but didn't.

"Fah what?"

"Just ... you know. Dress better. Mebbe we get di job, if wi clean up."

"For a job diggin trench and carryin steel and cement?" Jonesy was scornful. "Better dem see dis." He flexed his biceps and struck a pose.

"You too fool-fool. Mi a go change. Meet you at Miss Queenie?"

"No, mi will come wid you. Mebbe you len me a shirt."

"Nah fit you. You big now, man. Look like country yam did agree wid you."

Jonesey smiled. "Deena at home?"

"No. School."

"She okay?" Jonesey was close to Roy's daughter.

Roy didn't respond. Deena's asthma had been much better since the quarry had closed, but he still had an unfilled prescription in his pocket and a scrap of paper with the word NEBULISER scrawled on it from their last visit to the clinic in Harbour View. He *had* to get this job.

When the quarry was operating, Back To was covered in dust for most of the year. Dust coated every leaf, stone wall, roof, blade of grass, stand of wild cane, school desk, kitchen table, every human head that had been outside too long. Its sources were many – the quarry, a more distant mine, the bare playing field, unpaved roads, the river itself, a stream of trucks kicking up and transporting dust as they drove in and out. The elders of Back To spoke of a time before the mining and the quarrying when the river was a source of fresh water and abundant fish and no one had heard of asthma; but Roy knew the dust came from progress. His nose ran constantly, his sinuses throbbed and his eyes scratched, but dust was money. Dust caused Deena's asthma, and dust bought help for her too.

Men were already gathering in the yard of the community centre, and the parking lot was full of SUVs from Kingston. Two policemen stood at the gate. There was an empty space between the growing crowd and the shut front door, a no-man's-land of sorts.

"Wi need a contact inside," whispered Roy. That was how it worked. They needed someone who would get them to the top of the list, who would speak for them.

"Wait 'ere," Jonesy said. He always knew how to work the system.

Roy watched him swagger over to a browning with light eyes and tall hair, leaning against one of the SUVs, looking at her mobile phone. The waiting men of Back To murmured and kissed their teeth and shuffled their feet. Bully, Back To's official troublemaker, picked up a stone and threw it from hand to hand. The door to the community centre remained closed.

Roy heard a low whistle. Jonesy beckoned from the SUV.

"You memba Lisarelle from school?" he said. "She di new project liaison officer. She going put wi name at di top a di list."

Roy did not remember Lisarelle, who looked way too stush to ever have gone to school at the Back To All-Age. He felt the hot gaze of the waiting men on his back, and knew it would take very little for Bully to throw the stone. "Round the back," Lisarelle said to Jonesy. "Hurry up. You going get me inna trouble."

They walked around the dilapidated building and saw the back door was open. It was dark inside, and the room smelled of rat shit and human piss. Three men sat at a table facing the door; two were Chinese, and one was a brown man. *Chinese contractors, then. Not Mexicans.*

"Mawnin," Jonesy said to the brown man.

"Names?" the man snapped. "Lisarelle sent you?" *Jamaican,* Roy deduced, but not local. Probably uptown Kingston. Maybe army or police.

They both nodded. Jonesy gave their names, and the Jamaican wrote them in a large red book.

"Which part you from?" the brown man asked.

"Right yah so," Jonesy said. "Back To."

"You have construction experience?"

"Yeah, man. I mean, yes, sah. Whole heap." Jonesy rattled off an entirely fabricated work history, followed by a more truthful account of the various people in Back To he would be able to introduce them to.

The Jamaican raised his eyebrows. "When last you get work?"

Roy decided to speak up in case Jonesy told further lies, which would be too easy to check. "Last time dem fix di bridge, sah. When dem kinda patch-patch it up after di hurricane."

"So you don't work for close to two years?"

"Not steady. Likkle bit a dis and dat – help clear one field, clean drain, dat kinda t'ing. But no construction work dis side for a long time."

The Jamaican wrote in his book. He asked for their addresses and phone numbers. Roy watched the Chinese men, but they did not meet his eyes. They were sweating. They did not fidget or move in their chairs – he thought they would sit there forever if they had to, even if the community centre collapsed around them. He couldn't tell which one was the boss, and that unnerved him. Would they bring a Chinese work crew, or would there simply be Chinese bosses? How would the Jamaicans and Chinese people communicate? Even if they spoke English, they wouldn't speak

Jamaican, for sure. He heard the voices of the waiting men outside growing louder.

"Right. Monday morning onsite. Seven AM," said the Jamaican man. "If you late even one time – *one time* – you out. No weapon. Not even a ratchet knife. No drugs, including weed. No fighting. You see me?"

"Yes, sah," Roy said. "Thank you. You nah be sorry, sah."

Neither man asked about the pay.

The hiring lasted a single day, and the men of Back To gathered in the RenkanFacety bar that night to discuss who had been given jobs. The usual negotiations with the Member of Parliament had not occurred, and the security workers were all from Kingston. "Wi need di work!" snarled an older man known as Ranger. He was reputed to have had trade union experience back in the day. "What dem bring Chiney people here fah?"

"You see any ooman over dey?" said his sidekick, Fenton. "Who going clean and cook?"

"Different time now," said Maas Mac, one of Back To's elders, but his voice faltered. Roy stayed quiet. The men he had known all his life would find out he had been given one of the scarce jobs soon enough.

Bully went over to Ranger and leaned on the bar. "Mi is di Community Liaison Officer for di bridge work," he boasted. Mi can put in a good word for you, if you nah cause any commotion." He gestured to the barman to refill Ranger's drink and turned to face the room.

"Chiney people good boss, man. Evrybaddy going eat a food from dis, you see me?" Jonesy stood beside Bully, Ranger and Fenton, and they drank together.

That weekend, a dozen Chinese men moved into Back To. They found a flat piece of land deposited by one of the floods and erected a chain-link fence around it. Jonesy and Roy had never seen a fence built so quickly. The men swung their pickaxes and shovels together. They did not sing, they did not talk, they did not laugh. They were dressed in baggy trousers and long-sleeved shirts, orange high-visibility vests and hardhats, and they carried reusable bottles. They did not look tall or strong, but they did not rest. One man did not work – he carried no shovel or pickaxe. But he also gave no orders. He stood, chain-smoking, at one corner of the flat land, and he watched.

"You t'ink him is di boss?" Roy said.

Jonesy shrugged. "Look so. Mi no care who is boss, still."

"Mi care."

Three hours later the fence was finished, and the workers brought out flags with strange symbols on them and tied them to the corners. At lunchtime, they lined up along one end of the fenced area, lit cigarettes and drank from their bottles. A van came up and handed out boxes of food. They squatted close to the fence, took small sticks out of their pockets and used them to eat the food.

"Them coulda give Miss Lorraine di lunch contract," Roy said.

"Mebbe Chiney people don't like flour dumplin," Jonesey said.

By the end of the weekend, there was a work camp in Back To. Flimsy buildings had been erected overnight, long and thin and white, low-roofed with few windows, doors at each end. A large, open shed had been constructed, and it was full of tools and equipment with a small, enclosed office to one side. There was a line of bright blue portable toilets. Power and water had been connected. The gate into the fenced area was padlocked. The Chinese men disappeared into the low buildings at dusk.

"Me hear sey dem come from prison inna China," Roy told Jonesy.

"Bare chat," Jonesy answered.

That Sunday night, Roy couldn't sleep. He had never been nervous about a job before – it had always been a simple transaction. Manual labour in the sun, pay at the end of the week. Life easier for a while, then back to hustling. This time seemed different.

He heard the catch of Deena's breathing from the cot at the foot of his bed. He wished his sister in New York would send for his daughter. He could look after himself no matter what, job or no job – but Deena was slowly becoming the colour of Back To's dust, and that was a different kind of burden. That could crush a man. But he hardly heard from his sister anymore, and never from Deena's mother.

Why were the Chinese men in Jamaica, in Back To? Were there no jobs in their own country? Roy knew almost nothing about China, but he remembered a picture of a long wall snaking along a mountain ridge in one of his textbooks, described as one of the Seven Wonders of the World. He had thought it unremarkable, like the stone walls of Manchester he had seen on the one and only time he had ever left his parish. He had looked for Jamaica's wonders in the textbook, but there weren't any.

Roy got up when Maas Mac's rooster began to crow. He made himself a cup of mint tea with two spoons of condensed milk, and went outside where it was cooler. There was no hint of light in the sky.

Almost every man he knew wanted steady work. *Why had the government chosen Chinese workers? What would it be like, working for and alongside strangers, foreigners? Were more on their way? Less than twenty people could not build a bridge! Would the Jamaican workers get the food they had seen handed out?*

The first in a convoy of flatbed trucks went by, and he tasted dust. They lined up outside the gate to the worksite. He sat on a rock, drinking the cooling tea, steadying his mind. Then he went inside to get his daughter ready for school. He could perhaps bring home half his lunch for Deena, so he added a plastic bag to his backpack to prevent the spill of gravy. *Work is just work,* he reminded himself.

Five Jamaicans had been hired, not including Bully: one to open and shut the gate, one in charge of sweeping the site and three, including himself and Jonesy, as part of the work crews. Their first job was to unload the flatbed trucks. Two of the Chinese men walked the riverbanks with instruments and chose the site for the buttresses. They consulted with no one except each other.

"What in the boxes?" Roy asked Jonesy at the end of the first day.

Jonesey shrugged. "Mi just unload, like dem sey."

Roy's work crew was led by a boy who looked barely eighteen, called Kang. He was nicknamed "Kangaroo" by the Jamaicans, on and off the site, which was immediately shortened to "Roo" … and he did have a slight hop in his gait. He knew some English, but he rarely talked to anyone in any language, and Roy began to wonder if men building bridges needed to speak with each other after all. As he worked in an unaccustomed silence, he thought about how he and Jonesy never talked about Deena's illness, or how he came to be raising her alone, or of Jonesy's fight with the fisher, rumoured to be Jonesy's half-brother, or how a Red Stripe was good for filling an empty belly.

Once the flatbed trucks were unloaded, the Jamaicans were separated from each other and put into crews with the foreigners. Three bosses met every morning in the small office and planned the day's work. They came out and signalled to their teams – and the buttresses to support the new bridge, downstream of the old supports, began to rise. The Jamaicans were given phones that translated English into Chinese symbols, and they spoke into the phones and held them up to the bosses, who nodded but often ignored the suggestions of the Jamaicans. The Chinese did the same to communicate with Bully, who did not labour.

The bosses assembled the equipment the trucks contained, and Roy learned a new word: *cantilever*. It was a kind of formwork made of steel. The concrete mixers poured cement into the cantilever and the span of the bridge began to emerge, growing out from one riverbank like something alive, reaching. The work crews waited for the concrete to set before a new span was started, and then they switched to the other side of the river. Roy saw then how seventeen people – eighteen if you counted Bully – could build a bridge without words.

That summer, the hurricanes tracked north and south of the island and the pastors took the credit. He had never had such a long stretch of work, never eaten so well, and the nebuliser to help Deena's asthma sat in the corner of their room, plugged into the socket installed by Jonesy via an illegal connection to a utility pole. As the year wound down, the luminous December light softened the edges of Back To, and the half-finished bridge seemed otherworldly, as if it had its own source of light. At Christmastime, he hung tinsel over the door to his house and bought Deena a new phone. The families of the men who worked on the bridge rented the community centre for Christmas dinner.

“Wi not invitin anybody else? Roy asked Jonesey.

“Anybody like who?”

Roy didn’t answer, but he knew Jonesey had understood. The Chinese were their co-workers … but not their friends. *Maybe dem don’t celebrate Christmas,* he thought.

The new year began, and the men still gathered in the RenkanFacety Bar in the evening. Opposition to the bridge had died away: even though the bridge was not finished, the quarry had been open for months, their trucks using the fording. Cookshops and bars were thriving, and all manner of small jobs had sprung up for the people of Back To. The women mended torn clothes, grew vegetables in old tires and raised chickens for the food that was cooked every day at the camp. Maas Len kept pigs and goats for weekend feeds, and even the sound-system men began to blast their music again. A few women grew bellies, and Roy and Jonesy speculated on what the babies would look like – straight or curly hair, white or brown skin – and whether or not they would ever see their fathers after the bridge was completed. Kang was one of those who was seen each evening walking beside Serena, who had been head girl of the Back To All-Age School. Her belly was round and high, and her eyes were prideful.

Roy began to look ahead to the day when the bridge would be finished.

"What going happen?" he asked Jonesey, who was now considered to be well connected with the bridge project high-ups.

"Dem going pull evryt'ing down," he said. "Lisarelle say dey just move on to a different place."

"Evryt'ing better since di bridge start build," said Roy. "Bridge better dan quarry."

"But is di quarry why di bridge build," objected

Jonesy. "You t'ink any pretty new bridge would build for Back To? Quarry need bridge, and bridge need quarry."

"Why wi can't mek a work crew like dis, move around Jamaica? Send money home to Back To?"

Jonesy shrugged. "Politricks. Dem call wi 'unskilled'. Mi no know."

"You put aside any savings? Throw partner?"

"Mi? No, sah. Mi have neider chick nor chile; mi drink, mi eat, mi smoke, mi fix up mi place, get new phone. Can't do nutt'n about what is to come."

As the March dry time was ending, the completion of the bridge dominated Roy's thoughts. When he watched Deena sitting on the front step of their house with her friends, playing with their new tablets, given out by the Chinese at a function the politicians came to, they were shaded by the shadow of the bridge. When he closed his eyes for sleep, he saw dust falling from the sky until the bridge was covered.

There was talk of layoffs, and a big launch fete with ministers of government from Kingston. Although there were traffic cones preventing entrance to the bridge, a few taximen threw them into the river and drove up onto the bridge just to show they could. They got out of their cars and raised their arms in triumph.

One evening after work, Roy walked alone to the river. The subtle camber of the bridge gave him a soaring feeling, and he felt small beside it. And proud. *Men* had built this, men with strong backs and powerful legs, men with new words sparsely used, like *camber* and *truss* and *cantilever*. Men with skills, wielding tools, machines. And what they had built was a marvel.

It was cool under the bridge. The river flowed over sand and rocks, and wild cane waved in the evening light. He sat on the base of one of the columns and eased off his work boots, remembering the day he had been able to buy them from the back of a pickup truck at the site. He slid his feet into cold, shallow water and listened to the clacking sound of small stones pulled toward the sea, and the swish of the wind through the cane. He remembered the night the bridge was torn away, when he feared he might drown with his daughter.

He heard footsteps and looked up. It was Kang, walking down the path. Roy raised his hand in greeting, expecting him to walk right past – because, surely, he was there for work. But the Chinese man walked right up to him and stopped. Their eyes met. Kang did not have his hardhat on, and Roy had not seen him bareheaded before. His hair was long and shiny, loose on his shoulders. His eyes were ackee seed black; his skin smooth and pinkish-brown after months in in the sun.

"I want your help," Kang said, and his voice was scratchy and low and hard to understand.

"Talk," Roy answered, although he wanted to point out that the workday was over.

"Your life," Kang said. "It is better because of the bridge. We see it."

Roy nodded, wondering where this was going. He had worked alongside Kang for a year, had seen him meet Serena when she was part of the lunch team, had watched her share out extra portions for Kang and touch his shoulder. Did he have family back in China? A wife, ageing parents, children? Did he live in a city, or out in the country? Did he have an education? Had he been somebody?

"It is better for everybody," said Kang.

"Don't you want to go back to China?" asked Roy, in standard English.

"China? No. Stay here. Here is better. And we know how. You and your friends help me blow up this bridge. Then we have to build it again."

Roy thought he must have misheard. "Blow up di raas bridge? But you lick you raasclaat head! Sum'n fall on you, Roo?"

Anger flashed in Kang's eyes and Roy saw he had registered the nickname, understood and resented it. "You." He pointed at Roy's chest. "*Think*. If we blow up the bridge, they have to build it again. Everybody have work. Things good for another year. Maybe longer."

"You serious? What you know about dynamite?"

"A lot. Built dams in China. Quarry have plenty explosives. Got it already. Bridge have four buttresses, that's all. Easy."

"Is a crazy idea, Kang. If we even do it, we will get ketch for sure. We die in jail."

"You. *Think*," Kang said again. "Talk to your friends. But soon." He lifted his gaze to the underside of the bridge he had laboured to build. Roy realised he had never seen him smile.

Kang's idea never left Roy's mind as plans for the upcoming launch were revealed. The people of Back To were excited, looking forward to visitors, the food, even the droning speeches of the politicians. Small clean-ups were started. Curbs and tree trunks were painted white. All Roy could think about was the bridge returning to dust. If they blew up the columns, wouldn't the span of the bridge just fall into the river and dam the water behind it? Did Kang really know what he was doing? Could he trust Jonesy with such a crazy scheme? Could he trust anybody?

Halfway through July, Roy was laid off. The brown Jamaican, Captain Foster, was back behind the desk in the community centre, and he gave Roy his final wages. "Any new work startin, boss?" Roy asked.

"Not here," Captain Foster said. "NEXT!"

Roy phoned Jonesy and asked to meet him at the wall overlooking Back To. The credit on his phone was nearly done. He stared at the bridge in the distance while he waited, and remembered how the elders called it "the bridge to nowhere". The year of construction, only some of which he had seen, spiralled in his mind: the quarrying of the limestone to make cement, the trucks to move the material, the steel formwork transported from across the sea, the big concrete mixers turning and turning, the bridge emerging. *So what if it was not eternal? So what if it was returned to the dust from which it had come? Who could say that was wrong?* The bridge could be built and rebuilt and destroyed over and over, and the people of Back To would benefit until the dusty white hills were themselves levelled. By then Deena would be a big woman; she would have outgrown her asthma, and perhaps they would have moved away.

Roy saw Jonesy coming up the road toward him. He staggered a little, and Roy knew he had been drinking. Then he saw him lift his hand in greeting, and a smaller figure walked up beside him: Kang. Then other men began to join them – five, ten, then almost twenty men,

Chinese and Jamaican, carrying boxes. The men from the work crews were in street clothes, their construction gear discarded.

Roy stood and raised his arms in celebration, like the taximen had done from the bridge itself. All they had to do was make sure no one was too close to the bridge over the Yallahs River when it was brought down, so it could emerge all over again.

# THE NIGHTWATCH

## MARY ROKONADRAVU

Years later, Poasa recounted the miracle of the bauxite mine – how this hole in the ground lifted him from poor cassava-farming villager to owner of a Toshiba washing machine, a green twelve-wick kerosene stove and a tin house in Navuni Settlement in Suva. He also found a wife: Elesi. *Alice* in English. *Elzz* on the street. She was a seer in the Church of the Living Waters. Could see evil spirits in the form of one-eyed roosters perched on the backs of people. Cast the evil spirits into stray dogs. Now a follower of American President Donald Trump and televangelists Paula White and Jesse Duplantis, experts in mass digital prayers as thousands phoned in to transfer money into bank accounts in exchange for miracles.

Reverend Elesi – for that was now his wife's

name – was still in the early stages of discussion for M-PAiSA transfers through Vodafone Fiji and Western Union for rural givers. But they were now preparing to move into a $3,000-a-month three-bedroom flat at Rifle Range in Vatuwaqa, a gift borne by their church's members.

They had come a long way. Their relationship had quietly transitioned since they had met under what churchgoers would deem 'seedy circumstances', behind the Vatuwaqa Bakery: he had paid for her services at ten dollars for a blowjob and five dollars for a hand-job. He liked her because she did not talk. He liked her more because she smelled of Colgate toothpaste. He found peace in the commercial transaction. There was no cheating. No one attempted to take anything from him. She worked to make him come in the sweet blackness of the hibiscus bush behind the Chinese bakery. She did not stop until he came. Took a sip from a bottle of tap water afterward. Pressed a clump of toothpaste into her mouth. Ran it along her gums and swallowed it with another swill of water. Pulled his underwear up. Zipped his trousers.

He thought of her endlessly. On the bus. In bed. During rugby matches on television. At RB Patel Supermarket in Laucala Beach. In the queue at ANZ Bank. Even in church. He fought erections. He was sure his dick would fall off. He dreamed of green tomatoes. A beached two-headed shark. An old woman eating hot yams. Sometimes the old woman had his detached dick in her hand. Shrivelled. Limp. His eyes opening to the morning chill of the tin-walled bedroom as the hag smacked it on a rock. Over weeks of dreaming, he assured himself he could interpret his own dreams: the green tomatoes, the beached shark and the old woman eating hot yams were signs of his discomfort, loneliness and pain. But he needed specific definitions of his self-diagnosed condition. He needed an oracle. The watchman at The House of Carpets next to the Government Printing Press told him of one in Kinoya, off a short feeder road behind the sewage treatment plant.

The old *daurairai*, the-one-who-sees, was gifted the standard one pack of Benson & Hedges 20s, a red lighter, a Crest No. 18 chicken, four kilos of flour and a kilo of *yaqona*. Poasa added Maggi noodles. The old man mixed a bowl of *yaqona*, put his wrinkled right hand into it and said Poasa needed a woman.

"But what do you see?" asked Poasa, peering into the bowl of mud-coloured *yaqona*. He was dying for a smoke and a shit.

"I see a snake," said the *daurairai*. "Not the whole snake. Just the head. There is a crack on the head of the snake."

"Where is the crack?"

"In the middle."

"*Magaitinamu!* You mean like a dick?"

"That's a sad dick," said the *daurairai*. "You will slowly die. If you don't satisfy your dick, it will turn inward and poke your heart. That'll kill you."

Poasa let out a hard fart, akin in decibel to the common Diwali firecracker known as "the woodpecker". A loud pop.

*"Caita!"* said the *daurairai. Fuck!*

The oily fish-and-chips frustration couched in his anal crevice since lunch at Nabua's Happy Garden Restaurant came out in a billowing plume.

Afterward, it was said Poasa farted because the *daurairai* had his thumb pressed on his arse. Not inside, but *on* it, with a little pressure. That Poasa had eaten roti and tuna curry at lunch. That the boys peeping through holes in the wall smelled it too. No one cared to question how the boys knew about the *daurairai's* thumb pressure. But Poasa did not care. He bought Jardine hair food for the hibiscus bush appointment. Plus a coconut-fragranced Palmolive shampoo for dry hair and ten kilos of long-grain rice for Elesi. She wept. She also moved in that night. This, to Poasa, was the greatest gift God had willed him. Poasa believed that, like Jesus, he had rescued and given new life to a Mary Magdalene.

• • •

His mother rode the dawn milk-truck into Suva on Saturday. She rode without river prawns to sell at the market. She did not even take *rourou* for her son, or his favourite: half-ripe plantains from the garden next to their cookhouse. Nor did she take the ripe pineapples on the border of their yam plantation. Hers was a factory-tight coil of galvanised anger in the pit of her stomach. Bracing to spring like a cornered dog. Her cousins had brought word of Poasa's marriage to a young sex worker from the squatter settlement in Navuni. She'd never been to the settlement, but was aware her son had leased two perches. Built a tin house. Strung electricity into his house with an extension cord from a power socket six houses away. His house was fed electricity from a retired PWD plumber's shack from six in the evening to midnight at the rate of fifteen dollars per week. There were a few sparks when it rained, but his faith in God was big. He was a praying man, and the wires were covered with the blood of Jesus. He painted the house in Dulux "Tall Ships" blue and several sheets of corrugated roofing iron he had bought from the Shiva Temple in Samabula. The old camphor-steeped *dhoti*-clad priest selling it at a discount. He used the last of his money from the Chinese mine lease for this. Then he got a job as a watchman at the Government Printing Press at Vatuwaqa.

The plan was that his mother would come on

fortnight-long to month-long sojourns in Suva. To wash his clothes. Cook lamb flap stews. Plant gardenias to keep the smell of the mangrove soil down in the evenings. He was to save up for a flush toilet to replace the pit he was using before he could bring his mother over. The plan was firm until Elesi winked at him.

Elesi stood sniffing glue outside the bakery. Poasa almost dropped the long loaf he was carrying. He walked away with as much dignity as he could muster. He felt her eyes on his back until he turned the corner into Viria East Road. By the time he inserted the key into the lock at the main gate of the printery, his feet were no longer on earth. He was flying. No woman had ever winked at him. He was in love. Full one thousand percent.

The next night he slowed his pace upon entering the bakery. She winked again and signalled ten dollars for a blowjob. The first time she braced herself against the hibiscus bush to take him in her mouth, he knew he wanted her to be the mother of his children. He had been, until then, a virgin.

He did not know they were quite visible to the bakery boys and Chong Toy, the old Chinese baker and owner of the business, from their first-floor washroom. The lightbulb had cracked, and they used the washroom in a shroud of darkness. They also had a good view of the hibiscus bush.

"Hey, Chong," one of the boys said the first night, "see Alice she fuck the watchman from Government Printing. In our hibiscus. They dinging there."

"What?" asked Chong through the cigarette dangling from his mouth. "What you say, huh?"

"Alice! She dinging there." The boy pointed to the hibiscus bush through the mildewed wall of the bakery.

"Who she ding-ding?"

"New guard. Government Printing."

When Chong pulled out the first batch of hot bread tins from the wood-fired oven late that night he saw a hard-baked, crusty brown penis with two perfect balls attached to it, an arrow pointing at a poor attempt at a vagina on one of the loaves. A few wormlike threads emerged from the scrotum.

The cigarette fell out of Chong's mouth as he cracked laughing. "Hey, we gonna put in to pay for this bread," he said afterward.

"If we pay, we eat it," said one of the boys. "You gonna eat the dick and the two ball. *Vosota,* only next time we gonna make the dick big – then you gonna get full!"

"Next time you make it, I gonna make you sit on it," said Chong, as he turned the pan over and the dick, balls and pubic hair fell onto the large wooden table.

• • •

Poasa's mother rode the dawn milk-truck into Suva. Her nephew Samuela drove for the Rewa Dairy Limited. He began his route at five in the morning, collecting from small dairy farmers dotted along the Waidewara flats, along the banks of the Waidina River in darkness. The truck's headlights illuminating thick mists. There was the lowing of cows. Hides warm to the hand. Bats gorged on low-hanging breadfruit. Once, Samuela had reached out and put his hand around a grown bat feeding thus. The creature shrieked, spreading its black wings wide. He never forgot how soft, how like silk it was, slipping out of his grasp. Its wild heart. Taut flesh. The rush of about one hundred other bats, wings pulsing in a mist-wet glide over the low forests of Serea. By first light, they would be tucked into their wings like oversized ebony cocoons hanging from the gnarled arms of middle-range trees under the forest canopy. Bellies full. Only juveniles rested late. Their young bodies new, learning the curve of the world, every slope and tilt of the Earth, bones learning the cold rising from rivers that ran as dark threads on the flat regions below. Their eyes suddenly blinded by the first rays of the sun. It took time to learn to home. When to abandon the lush temptation of a red mango. The call of a bursting jackfruit. The tug of a cluster of sweet papayas. How to smell the turn of night.

Samuela turned to tell his silent aunt about the bat, then quickly held his tongue. She was seated tight as a soldier at drill: stomach in, chest out, shoulders back and down, hands glued to the side, no daylight between the arms and the body. He knew it would take Poasa some effort to ease her. He did not envy his cousin the task. He looked into the mist and whistled a gospel tune. At Valelevu, about a kilometre before the Rewa Dairy factory, he put her in a taxi. Slipped twenty dollars into her green handbag.

Poasa was an only son. His mother came with a mission. When she reached Navuni, she was welcomed with the smell of rotting uncollected rubbish that stood at the end of the street. She gagged. Quickly paid the driver. Sought directions from a child of about twelve.

"Do you know a man called Poasa?"

"Poasa the fisherman, or Poasa married to the *kalavo*?"

*"Kalavo?"* asked Poasa's mother with a straight face.

"Yes, *kalavo*. The rat. Everybody calls the woman that, and she's married to the second Poasa. Rats make money on the street, that's what my mother says."

"Take me to the second Poasa."

Her son's house stood at the edge of the

mangroves. His share of eleven thousand dollars from the Chinese mining company was transformed into a tin shack on a marsh. Mangrove stumps protruded dangerously from the swamp. Old car tires retrieved from a dump were lined into a makeshift walkway to the house. Her eyes could tell he had put the house together. He had no expertise in carpentry. The piles were high. Crooked. Thin wood posts fashioned out of mangrove trunks. There was no squaring or levelling. It was a patchwork of wood and tin nailed one over the other. The windows were holes in the walls. He had cut out sheets of the thick plastic the Toshiba washing machine came in and nailed these to the windows.

The front door was from a public convenience. MEN, it said in bold black paint. With the Fijian translation, TAGANE. The message TP 50 CENTS was followed by an arrow pointing to the right. Unknown to her at the time was the fact that the back door said WOMEN, with the translation YALEWA. The same message about the sale of toilet paper at fifty cents. The lady in the booth rolled three times around her fist and tore portions. If you were to have a shit, you prayed a large woman with a huge fist was in, or you would buy two to three portions. Poasa had not bothered cleaning the doors. A few streaks of aged, matted brown were at the centre of the door. The section around the handle was also a matted black. Heaven knew how many thousand hands had touched this piece of wood. How many unwashed after holding their penises over urinals. How many unwashed after changing their sanitary napkins in toilet stalls. How many unwashed fingers with dollops of faeces that cut through the thin paper.

• • •

She thought of the old but sturdy house her husband had built from the sweat of his brow, harvesting truckloads of yams and *dalo*. He paid the Indian carpenter, Ambika Prasad, to come up to the village for two months to raise the house from the ground. Theirs was the first house in the village to have bedrooms – three spacious ones. Two beds and a kitchen cupboard had also been made from the leftover wood. She thought of the water-seal toilet that was required to be twenty metres away from the main house and the cookhouse. Unlike most homes that used offcuts of wood and tin to build a toilet as an afterthought, Ambika Prasad, seeing how she cleaned out and aired their current toilet, lay a good concrete foundation for the new one, installed the standard rural design bowl from the Ministry of Health and put up a tight tongue-and-groove wall. Well ahead of its time, before any house in the capital, this toilet had a river pebble floor; Ambika Prasad carted loads of pebbles and set them into the soft concrete. He brought rocks and created a lush corner for wild ferns potted in cleaned paint tins. She thought of the *uci* plants her mother-in-law had encouraged her to plant around it to freshen the air. Keep the Evil Eye at bay. Three *mokosoi* trees planted behind the house, for the scenting of coconut oil and the breeze around the house. The cold mountain river plunging down basalt rocks. The steam of a chilled world rising from the surface. From patches of the river under the shade of dense forest foliage, cold steam rose even from the speckled surface in the hottest sun. She almost closed her eyes.

Almost.

But here she was at the edge of a degraded salt swamp. There was an incoming oil-sheened tide carrying in plastic bottles, plastic bags and half-opened rubbish bags with refuse, rotting leaves and soiled diapers with stagnant hosts of buzzing flies. Above this tide, her son was asleep with a sex worker. She was sure of it. Her urge to berate her son gave way to the urge to clean this rising filth. She saw an old *sasa* broom tucked into the remains of a pandanus mat. They were thrown carelessly over a makeshift rail on a porch that could barely seat two grownups. She placed her green handbag under the mat and took the broom. She swept out the old tires, extracting bottles and tin cans from within. By the time she reached the saltwater edge, eleven children, the youngest about four years old, had joined. The youngest ones were a snot-nosed crew but eager to pull, push, pick and carry rubbish to a dry patch of land nearby.

A woman appeared from somewhere with a couple of old FMF flour sacks. Another group began carting rubbish to the main road where the Suva City Council collectors made one pick-up in the week. Cans and bottles were easy enough to handle. The soiled baby diapers were another story. She used a flat piece of wood to push them along the water toward land, where the older children used sticks to lift them into flour sacks. The place was beginning to take on a cleaner look. She turned to thank the woman when the door suddenly opened, and her son stood there with a cane knife. Struck it against the tin wall.

*"Ei!"* he shouted, *"Ei! Lako tani! Dou lako tani!" Go! Go away!*

The children scattered like startled chickens.

"Poasa. *Luvequ*," she said. *My son.*

*"Na! Na!" Mother!* He shouted. *"Na cava o mai cakava? O lialia tiko?" What are you doing here? Are you mad?* His voice rose to a shriek when a woman's voice rose from within the blue shack.

"Hallelujah! Hallelujah! Jisu! Jisu!"

She watched her son quieten, making way for

his three-day-old wife emerging from the dark shack.

"Spirit of jealousy!" she screamed, "Spirit of jealousy is here! Jisu! *Turaga*!" The young woman's long crimson nails pointed at Poasa's mother. "Wrong spirit! I command you to come out in Jesus's name! Out! Out! Out! Jesus!"

Poasa's mother stood transfixed. She watched her son throw his head back and rock.

"Jesus! Jesus!"

But it was the young woman that her eyes rested upon. She was quite dark, and her frizzy hair had been straightened with a hot iron. Her hair could be mistaken for an avian life form, a parrot or a cockatoo. Emerald, crimson and a rich purple streak brightened her head. Lipstick and mascara were smeared from sleep, neither washed off from the previous night. Or for several days. One could not tell. She was wearing a short skirt. Her stomach protruded from under the lime spaghetti-strap blouse struggling to contain her bosom. Nipples hard.

"Don't judge!" the woman shouted. "Spirit of judging in your eyes! Don't judge! Don't judge!

*Vosoti koya, Turaga! Forgive her! Forgive her, Lord!* In the name of Jesus!"

The truth was that Poasa's mother, and indeed the rest of the neighbours, could not do anything, let alone have a coherent thought. Another woman emerging from the row of houses behind Poasa's mother walked forward with a kitchen knife.

"Hey! *Saqamua*! What happened to you? You climb Poasa last night and turn into a preacher? His dick turn you into an evangelist? You think we born yesterday?"

"Lord, forgive them!" cried out Elesi. "*Vosoti ratou!* Hallelujah! Glory!"

*"Oy!"* shouted the knife-wielding woman. "Last night you suck Poasa behind the bakery! What? You scared of Poasa's mother now? Don't pretend to be holy-holy! *Qara levu*!"

*"Au revevaka ga na Kalou!"* Elesi shouted. *I only fear God!* "Who is this woman who just came today? I don't know her!" She took the green handbag and flung it.

Poasa's mother retrieved the bag from the water. All the words she had brought along with her sat mute under her tongue. Her eyes were on her son, who was now speaking a language she could not understand.

"See! My husband is now speaking in tongues! *Vinaka Turaga! Emeni! Emeni!*"

A crowd had gathered, and there was laughter all around. Many were filming the spectacle on smartphones. Some, livestreaming on Facebook.

*"Oy!"* came a shout from within the crowd. "How do we know Poasa is speaking God's message? Who will interpret?"

"I will!" said Elesi. "The message is for all of you stubborn unbelievers! Repent and return to God! Or the fires of Hell will burn this city! The Lord is angry!"

"Wait!" cried out another voice from the crowd. "What does God say about Poasa's dick?"

Elesi mumbled something and the crowd roared.

Poasa's mother slowly inched into the crowd. Retraced her steps to the end of the street. She had seen fights and disagreements in the village. Nothing like this. Walking slowly down the mud path, she inched her way between lines of homes built in the manner of her son's. There were both Indians and Fijians, and those of mixed race. There was no piped water. Electricity was stolen from the FEA posts on the main street and fed into several homes, which then sub-fed others. She saw extension cords snaking through houses, trees, and pinned to old forty-four-gallon diesel drums. The smell of wet mangrove mud blended with animal and human faeces was thick in the air. She walked a little faster. Upon reaching the end of Navuni, she continued toward Fletcher Road. She was sweating now. Needed water.

Turning a corner, she saw a little bakery. CHONG TOY BREAD SHOP. There was a small retail section. The entire frontage was taken up by advertisements for Vodafone and Digicel recharge cards, Punja's Flour, Coca-Cola, Sprite, Fanta and Pepsi. The bakery was deserted. She stepped inside. She was greeted with the smell of fresh bread – a reminder of her husband, Poasa's late father, who bought several loaves after every sale of root crops in Suva or Nausori. He always kept about three loaves for them. Shared the other loaves with his uncles and cousins. She quickly pushed the thought aside. A radio crackled. The volume low. There was a fiery preacher speaking brimstone against homosexuals. She stood quietly, waiting for someone to see her.

The bakery boys were asleep upstairs, but Chong and two boys were cooling themselves under the ceiling fan in the bakery section, which was curtained off. They saw the elderly woman, Poasa's mother, in the high ceiling mirror. She was in a bright hibiscus *sulu* and *jaba* that reached her ankles. Her hair was combed out neatly in the traditional Fijian *buiniga*. She carried a green handbag. She was obviously not from the neighbourhood. Chong sent Akuila, one of the better-smelling boys with a neater haircut, to serve her.

*"Bula, Nau,"* Akuila said.

"Forgive me," Poasa's mother said. "Can you please give me a glass of water? And do you have a place I can sit at for a little while? I only need to rest for a few minutes. Then I'll go."

It was a strange request. Akuila was about to defer to Chong, when he called out from the back room.

*"Mai! Mai!" Come!*

Chong freed a wood bench in the coolest part of the room. Akuila followed with a glass of water. It was a strange affair. They had never been visited by such a well-dressed Fijian woman. She was elderly. Regal in appearance. Dignified. Akuila took a *sasa* broom and began sweeping out dust and flour. Chong sat opposite her.

"*Nau*, we make the tea for you. You eat some bread, too." He sent Peni, the second boy, up to fetch clean plates and cutlery. Afterward they would agree that none knew why they behaved thus, but here they were, making the woman comfortable. By the time Chong and the boys spread a clean tablecloth, set the cutlery and brewed tea, the woman was in tears.

*"Vinaka! Vinaka!"* she kept repeating. *Thank you!*

Chong watched the two boys slip to the back. He reached into a cupboard next to him and brought out a clean hand towel, one the boys used during the night shift. The woman wiped her tears. She sat quietly, Chong's hand on her back. Then she quietly sipped tea. She wanted to talk, but Chong signalled her not to.

So here they were, sitting, when the radio suddenly came alive and they heard a flurry of footsteps in Fletcher Road. The boys asleep upstairs came running down.

"Hey! There's another coup! The gang marching in town, they going to Parliament and taking over!"

The other boys knew the routine, and worked fast. They ran outside and pulled the barbed gates shut, slipped a large padlock to lock it down. Several padlocks, in fact. This was not the first military coup. By the time they came in to shut the doors and barricade the windows from looters, people from the settlement were running with rocks and grabbing handfuls of gravel to fling at Indian taxi drivers and at Indian homes. They already knew that not a single taxi or private vehicle would stop for anyone. The capital would be emptying fast. One of the boys ran upstairs to switch on the television.

Mass looting was already underway. RB Patel Supermarket on upper Waimanu Road was being ransacked by civilians. Cartloads of liquor and frozen chicken and lamb chops were being rolled out its entrance. Two separate sections of the city were burning. There was a shop owner weeping on the main street. Young boys ran up and down Victoria Parade beating and punching Indian drivers for no reason. The reporter and the cameraman reporting the news were in tears. The reporter kept on talking through his tears until a shower of rocks hit their vehicle. They left the camera rolling. In front of the television, the youngest of the bakers, fifteen-year-old Jemesa, was in tears, and he did not even know why.

Chong and his boys ran to check on their fire extinguishers. They had three. They checked the taps. Water was running, and the boys began collecting it in their largest buckets and containers. But they stared at Chong.

"See? We tell you to buy the generator, but you want to keep your money!"

They were still talking when someone crashed

through the bushes. Rushed in through the back door. It was an Indian taxi driver. His taxi was burning on Fletcher Road. One of the boys took his hand and got him to sit beside their lady visitor.

It was then that they realised that she was very still. Her head a little forward. Chong pried her fingers from her empty cup of tea and held her hand. He held her hand in his and wept like a child. The Indian taxi driver wept. The boys clutched the wooden table in the far corner of the bakery, their shoulders heaving.

It was silent in the bakery that night. As the fires died down and orange embers lit a city in darkness, Chong, the boys and the Indian taxi driver settled in to sit the night out. They had gone out in the early evening, placing the Fijian woman in the bread van. For the first time, Chong did not drive. He held her in his lap. He and the youngest, Jemesa. The Indian taxi driver drove them to the CWM Hospital, to the mortuary. Chong had her handbag. He found her nephew's work number. He would call the next day. On the way back, the Indian taxi driver realised he had urinated in his pants earlier that morning. He was dry now, but the smell hit his nostrils hard. Chong gave him a change of clothes. Soap to shower. A towel.

For now, they sat. Unsure whether or not they would be looted or burnt in the night. FEA shut electricity down on the whole island. The taps were dry. Only police and military vehicles moved around slowly.

"We alive, eh?" Chong whispered, "Good we alive."

In the settlement, a new prophetess was being hailed by its residents. After all, as she had predicted, the city *did* burn. Beside her, Poasa wept.

In the bakery, the motley men sat chewing bread in the darkness. Nothing moved. Every now and then a smoke-filled wind blew from the southeast. Their bodies tensed to sense approaching fire. Then relaxed. Only red and pink embers glowed in several charcoaled shops in Suva. Bats from the State House had flown across the city skyline hours earlier, high above the black smoke.

The peninsula was silent.

# AUTHOR BIOGRAPHIES

**Ntsika Kota**
**(OVERALL WINNER**
**AND REGIONAL WINNER: AFRICA)**
Born in Mbabane, Eswatini, Ntsika Kota is a chemist by training. A self-taught writer, he was originally inspired by a high-school writing assignment. His work is a reflection of his thoughts and feelings, and he enjoys creating that reflection.

**Sofia Mariah Ma**
**(REGIONAL WINNER: ASIA)**
Sofia Mariah Ma is a Singaporean writer. She recently placed second in the 2021 Golden Point Award, and published a short story, "The Forgetting", in the cli-fi anthology *And Lately, the Sun*. She holds an MA in English Literature, examining the works of Kazuo Ishiguro and his experimentations with genre. Currently, she is

working on a young adult novel inspired by her Javanese origins.

**Cecil Browne**

**(REGIONAL WINNER: CANADA AND EUROPE)**

Cecil Browne was born in St Vincent and the Grenadines, but has lived in the UK since his teens. A college lecturer in Maths for over thirty-five years, he loves cricket, writing and music. His short story, "Coming Off the Long Run" was published in the *So Many Islands* anthology in 2018. He has just finished writing his debut novel.

**Diana McCaulay**

**(REGIONAL WINNER: THE CARIBBEAN)**

Diana McCaulay is a Jamaican environmental activist and writer. She has written five novels – *Dog-Heart*, *Huracan*, *Gone to Drift*, *White Liver Gal* and *Daylight Come*. She was the Caribbean regional winner of the Commonwealth Short Story Prize in 2012, for "The Dolphin Catchers". She sits on the editorial board of *Pree*, an online magazine for Caribbean writing.

**Mary Rokonadravu**

**(REGIONAL WINNER: THE PACIFIC)**

Mary Rokonadravu is a Fijian writer of mixed indigenous Fijian, indentured Indian and settler European heritage. She won the Commonwealth Short Story Prize for the Pacific region in 2015, and was shortlisted in 2017. Her short stories have been published by *Granta* and *adda*, and have been included in anthologies by the University of London Press and Penguin Random House New Zealand (Vintage).

# Selected Titles from Paper + Ink

**I Cleaned the – & Other Stories: Winners of the Commonwealth Short Story Prize 2021**

**The Great Indian Tee and Snakes & Other Stories: Winners of the Commonwealth Short Story Prize 2020**

**Emissaries: Stories and Reflections**
*Dean William Rudoy*

**In Dreams: The Very Short Works of Ryūnosuke Akutagawa**
*Selected and Translated from the Japanese by Ryan Choi*

**Million-Story City: The Undiscovered Writings of Marcus Preece**
*Edited by Malu Halasa and Aura Saxén*

**Another Man**
*Leslie Croxford*

**The Dead**
*James Joyce*

**The Overcoat**
*Nikolai Gogol*
*Translated from the Russian by Constance Garnett*

**Bartleby, the Scrivener**
*Herman Melville*

**Independence Day & Other Stories**
*Pramoedya Ananta Toer*
*Translated from the Indonesian by Willem Samuels*

**In the Shadow of Death**
*Rūdolfs Blaumanis*
*Translated from the Latvian by Uldis Balodis*

**The Necklace & Other Stories**
*Guy de Maupassant*

www.paperand.ink